Island Girl

Born in the Netherlands, Lolo Houbein gained her B.A. Degree in the literatures of Ancient Greece and Rome, England and Australia, as well as Anthropology, at the University of Adelaide. She has an M.A. Qualifying degree in Pacific and African literatures from the University of Papua New Guinea and a Graduate Diploma in Teaching.

Some of her books and stories have won awards and her stories, columns and essays appear in anthologies and periodicals. She has travelled widely and her writing is inspired by other cultures.

Also by Lolo Houbein

One Magic Square: Grow Your Own Food on One Square Metre (Wakefield Press, Adelaide 2008)

Tibetan Transit (Kangaroo Press / Simon & Schuster, Sydney 1999) Travel, history, pilgrimage.

Lily Makes A Living (Hodder Headline, Sydney 1996) Young adult novel. Commended for the Jim Hamilton Award.

The Sixth Sense (University of Queensland Press, Brisbane 1992) Short stories. New edition of *Everything is Real*.

Wrong Face in the Mirror: An Autobiography of Race and Identity (University of Queensland Press, Brisbane 1990)

Vreemdeling in de Spiegel: Autobiografie van een Nederlandse Emigrante (Balans, Amsterdam 1988) Dutch translation of *Wrong Face in the Mirror.* Awarded the Dirk Hartog Literary Award.

Walk A Barefoot Road (ABC Books, Sydney 1988) Awarded the ABC-Bicentennial Fiction Award. Dramatised in eighteen episodes for ABC National Radio and transcribed into Braille. (Second edition, Middle Hill Books, 1990)

Everything Is Real (Phoenix Publications, Brisbane 1984) Short stories.

Also: *A Bibliography of Australian Multicultural Writers*, Compiled by Sneja Gunew, Lolo Houbein, Alexandra Karakostas-Seda and Jan Mahyuddin (Centre for Studies in Literary Education, Deakin University Press, Geelong 1992, and available on the Australian Literature Database)

Island Girl

Lolo Houbein

HYBRID
PUBLISHERS

Published by Hybrid Publishers
Melbourne Victoria Australia

First published 2009

National Library of Australia Cataloguing-in-
Publication entry:

Author: Houbein, Lolo, 1934–
Title: Isand Girl / Lolo Houbein

ISBN: 9781876462888 (pbk.)

Target Audience: For juveniles

Dewey Number: A823.3

Cover art 'Island Girl' © Suzie Riley

Printed in Australia by McPherson's Printing Group

Contents

For Robyn

1: A Skeleton called Flora

'And doesn't she have the features of Flora Hammermeyer,' says old Mrs Ivy Rutt as she waits for her groceries to be loaded into her pick-up truck. Her unsmiling, pale eyes run all over me like a search light, but she's not risking eyeball to eyeball contact. I shiver involuntarily. 'Same straight nose, arched eyebrows and those high cheekbones,' she continues. 'And that determined chin too.'

She means I look foreign.

Displeased, Mum nods and turns away without replying. What's going on? I've always imagined that at least my face was my own, even unique! Never met anyone with a face like mine. Out of the corner of my eyes I watch Ivy Rutt climb behind the wheel and settle her stiff back. Before starting the engine she calls down to Mum: 'Don't forget the district nurses trading table tomorrow, Kathy. Your pink icing biscuits always sell!'

'Will do, Ivy,' Mum mutters while putting petrol into our old bomb car. She hates being called Kathy. She once told us she never listened to that name any more after she left school. And who would, with a terrific name like Katinka?

Gary comes out of the Bay Shop with our supplies on a trolley, puts the boxes in the boot, shuts it, then gives the top a rap. We take off in the opposite direction to old Ivy, into the late afternoon sun. Our island's only main road runs east to west.

'Who is Flora Hammer …?' I ask as soon as we are coursing in top gear.

'Your great-grandmother,' Mum replies curtly.

So how come I am nearly eighteen and never heard of her?

'Dad's grandma then?' I insist. Because Mum's family all have misspelled Russian-sounding names. 'So what happened to Flora Hammer … whatever?'

'Hammermeyer. That was her married name, from Arend Hammermeyer. He wasn't an islander. Nor was she. He was Nordic or thereabouts.'

So that was it. They weren't islanders but main-landers, or immigrants. I was no more than five or six when Great-grandpa Arend died.

'Why isn't there anyone of that name left on the island?

'They had a son, but he went away and never came back.' Typical. Too many islanders head for the mainland and that's the last you see of them.

'So how come we are Woodsman if we descend from the Hammermeyers?'

'Your Grandma Barbara was their only other child and she married John Woodsman. That's all there is to that.'

No use asking further. Or is it? Mum's more than usual reluctance to answer questions makes me suspect there's a skeleton in Dad's family's cupboard.

A skeleton called Flora. Great-grandpa Arend's name is carried on by my big brother, but I never knew he had a wife. As a little kid I obviously didn't connect that if Grandma Barb was his daughter, then there must have been a mother!

Perhaps Tom Baudin knows. Not his real name, although Tom may be authentic. I did my oral history project on him last year. He adopted his surname from the first French explorer who came to these islands just after Matthew Flinders claimed them for the king of England. He is a hermit, but after the initial shock at getting a visitor, he said he didn't mind me dropping by for a yarn. He's ancient, over eighty, and knows lots of old stories about Platypus Island people.

Mum pulls up at the crossing where we'll have a ten minute wait for the schoolbus, but it will save the littlies wading through puddles. Our farm track got badly flooded by the southern squall that came through at noon.

It still feels weird to be out of school. Most of my friends are on Kangaroo Island or the mainland where the cadetships and part-time jobs are. Some work on family farms, quite a few are doing nothing, youth unemployment being much more here than the state-wide percentage. Only Sylvie is repeating her final year to improve her scores, as she still hopes to go to university.

I'm not sorry I stayed home when Mum needed

help to recover from breast cancer, but that was last year. Us five kids plus invalid Auntie Branka are a lot to look after. And Dad claimed that with the world becoming unsafe in the most unexpected places nowadays, he didn't want me to go off anywhere until things bottomed out and I had some idea of what I wanted to do and why and where. I didn't quarrel with that either. But nine months into this year, Mum seems tired of having me constantly around. And much as I love her, I too want out!

We don't communicate well lately. Shall I cause a storm by breaking it to her, or take advantage of a storm when she loses her cool about some little thing? Or shall I write a sweet little note: 'Dear Mum, I love you but I want to leave home to have a life of my own. No hard feelings. I will visit a lot.' Sounds ridiculous. She'd be offended. Besides, she'll probably argue I'm still too young to leave home and what will I do for money?

Leaving home immediately isn't really a priority, just a piece of a larger pattern I'm trying to work out. First priority is getting out of this endless housework. After years of school and homework with farm work to boot, freedom was beckoning with just housework and a bit of gardening. I thought I'd have oodles of free time. But it has turned out to be a daily drag. How has Mum put up with it for twenty years? She wasn't always depressed like she seems to be these days.

Trouble is I can't figure out what to do with my life

on my own, although in my mind I know precisely what I want. I want to do everything that interests me, but I have to narrow that down to something Mum and Dad will think sensible. Like doing a correspondence course in something that leads to a job, or trying my luck again at Parks & Wildlife – put my name down this time. But Mum will still want me to be on hand for the summer season. And in my heart of hearts I want to stay around in case my romantic friend returns, because I have thought about him on and off since he left last summer to do first year uni.

Mum clears her throat. 'If I put the ingredients in a bowl, you could mix and roll a batch of biscuits to bake tonight. I will ice them in the morning and Dad and Arend can drop them off when they go to footy training.'

'Okay,' I say. Don't mind baking biscuits. She's got it all worked out. All her mind does is organise the housework, half the farm work, us kids, our clothes and shoes and what the littlies need for school. Plus every request that Ivy Rutt or other organisers of other people's time – Auntie Branka's phrase – put to her for biscuits, cakes, or produce. When she looks at us she doesn't see us, but the clothes we're growing out of. Mentally she always sits at the sewing machine, although she hardly gets to it once a week. Does she ever think of anything else but work? What is she thinking of now?

The yellow schoolbus looms up in the rear vision mirror. It stops right behind us and Klaus the driver tries to kiss our rear bumper with the front of his bus to give us a little jolt. That's the sort of jokes people play on Platypus. Nothing better to do. Out tumble chubby Coral and Zora and skinny Yvan.

I don't know what got into Mum and Dad when they started an ABC of children: first Arend, then me. Mum wanted to name me after Auntie Branka, but Dad said: 'No way, Tinka. The kid won't like it when she grows up.' So she changed one letter: Bianka. Then came Coral. Sometimes we're good friends, but she's only in Year Ten. I once asked Mum and Dad how they knew they were only going to need two more letters of the alphabet when they named Yvan. It's not the way anybody spells that name and he always has to explain: 'Like Yvonne, but I'm a boy and I'm Yvan.' Zora has just turned ten. They bundle into the backseat.

Dad said they'd had a ten-year plan, but abolished it on account of Mum having her hands full with us three. They didn't realise Yvan was coming until he was nearly due and Mum called him Ivan after her dead uncle. But then another baby came unannounced. Is that possible? Did they mean unplanned? They decided she had to be the last, the Z that closed the alphabet. And so Ivan's name was adjusted. Poor guy has been confused ever since, but he's a great kid.

I once said they should have had one more child

with a name starting with X – to make a family from ABC to XYZ. Mum groaned and Dad laughed. 'Xantippe,' he shouted and told the story of the wife who drove her husband onto the streets of Athens thousands of years ago, until he was picked up for corrupting Greek street kids with his rebellious talk and made to drink poison until death set in. Gruesome. Dad is full of myths and legends; I love dipping into his books. He even has original copies of Jane Austen, a bit of a slow read due to people's good manners in that age. I wouldn't want to be like those women, lifelong spinsters or a man's possession. Nor do I want to be like Mum. How shall I organise my life so that I can do the things I love doing?

Splash! The suspension groans as we hit the biggest puddle with a crash-bang shower of mud. Our loyal dog Dreadlocks runs circles around the car. 'Get down, Dreads! You're filthy! No Jumping!' He barks and runs more circles, happy we're home again.

In the house we disperse. The littlies change into tracksuits to save their school clothes. They must do homework before they can play. Yvan does his on the computer, his favourite toy. Mum puts on the kettle to make tea for herself and Auntie Branka and stirs milo for the kids. I put the groceries away on the pantry shelves, take two biscuits for my troubles and step into rubber boots by the back door to go and feed my flock.

The geese, ducks and chooks squabble over the

grain, so I put out one bowl for the geese and one for the ducks, who can't easily eat from the ground, being fishers. I sprinkle a handful for the chooks in another corner of the run where Romeo the Gorgeous holds court. I watch them for a while. Rooster Romeo bows and scrapes, then makes dinner invitation noises. When his hens gather around he makes love to Rosie, his favourite big black chook, before they all peck away to fill their crops before turning in. They'll be roosting by five o'clock on this dark day.

I can think clearer in the chookrun than in a house full of people. When Mr. Antonini asked me in Year Eleven what I liked doing most, I said: 'Thinking.' He didn't seem surprised. 'You will be a philosopher then,' he said, smiling a sad smile. 'And wouldn't it be nice if you could think for a living?' I've never forgotten, because he was usually cheerful. He left for Kanga to teach at Kingscote, then back to the mainland. Did he want to be a philosopher himself? Or did he mean I was going to waste my talents? He always talked about each of us having at least one talent and we should organise our lives so that we could fully develop it. 'Don't become island-bound,' he would rave, mowing his long arms through the air. 'The world is waiting for your talent!' Yeah.

My talent. Whatever it is. Here in the run I can sit on my heels and dream a bit before it is time to cook dinner. Dream of my romantic friend who just might return for the season. Maybe I will tell him the secret name that I use when I go adventuring in my mind. Where else can I go adventuring these days? Mum would wonder what I'd be up to if I went to the cliffs too often, or took a bus to Queenscape without her shopping list. I haven't been anywhere for months except the Bay Shop and Sylvie's place.

Queenscape is my favourite travel destination, population four hundred. The eastern part of the island is like another world. You can see it broke off there from big, beautiful Kangaroo Island, which even in winter is cluttered with tourists – a world where I am a stranger. And where the jobs are.

As for the mainland, that's overseas, even though from the farm we can see the southernmost light-house blink on clear nights. I would have loved to be alive when Gwondanaland started to break up into continents and big and small islands. Imagine waking up one morning and finding yourself separated from your pet kangaroo, who is grazing in a paddock now across the water while you sit on a newly formed island with the platypussies!

Shall I tell him about my now-you-see-it-now-you-don't Sometime Island? Will he understand what it means to me, why I spend all my spare time there without leaving home? Or will he want to shut me up by trying to kiss me, as he did last summer behind the cliff, just before he and his family were leaving?

I've been thinking a lot about that kiss that didn't quite happen because a big wave suddenly crashed onto the rocks. Then the tide came in fast and we had to clamber quickly along the foot of the cliff to the beach or we would have been stuck there for the night. Drenched we were and darkness came down like a curtain. I ran home to keep warm. He could easily have caught up with me, but he didn't. So I'm seventeen and never kissed by a boy.

Bit of a record if you believed the goss at school and sports. Now I hardly see any boys apart from my brothers. I don't mind. Boys can be pretty stupid unless you know them really well. The big cup gum shadowing the chook run is flowering in clouds of creamy pink. As the setting sun shines through them, the buds look as if on fire. It's getting cold. I hear Arend getting wood for the stove. Dad will be home soon from the sales yard.

Tonight I am going to draw an adventure suit, a pair of overalls with thousands of pockets for essential equipment. Then I'll draft a pattern and one day I will cut and sew it. Ready for the day I disappear to a place like Sometime Island.

Goodnight Romeo, look after your harem. In the vegetable garden I activate the electric fence to keep out cheeky possums. This is my domain, an ancient vegetable garden that has fed the Woodsmans for more than a hundred years. I took over from Mum, whose arm is still too sore for gardening, because I just love growing things. Look at my cauliflowers all coming on at once! I cut the biggest for tonight with the knife stuck into the ground near the worm farm. A quick and easy meal. I will half cook it, then put it in the oven covered with butter and grated sheep cheese. Yum! I pick oregano, parsley and rosemary for pumpkin mash and run to the house. Been dreaming too long.

'No eggs?' asks Mum the minute I come in. She's a computer with flawless memory. I dash out to collect six eggs, sliding through the mud with three in each hand as the rain comes down again.

Staring out the kitchen window as I run the tap over the cauli to flush out slugs, I see Dad drive up. He looks zonked. It's been a rough year for him and Mum. Mum's illness cost a lot of money in fares to and from the mainland. Wouldn't it be nice if I could earn a wage and help them out a little? I put the pot on the stove, light the oven and start dicing pumpkin. Mum has peeled potatoes and I made rice pudding this morning, so we're almost done.

'How are all my favourite people?' thunders Dad, stomping into the livingroom in his socks. He is amazing. Never lets on that he's tired or worried. The littlies yell 'hello Dad' from their rooms and Dad kisses Mum behind my back. Then he puts a hand on my shoulder: 'How's my girl? Been busy?'

'Yep,' I say and give him a quick one on his stubbled cheek. I'll ask him about Flora once we've eaten.

When I do, after collecting Auntie Branka's plate from her room and washing the dishes, he is sitting in his easy chair with his feet on another chair and Mum is in Zora and Coral's room, organising them.

'Dad, tell me about your Grandma Flora Hammermeyer?'

He sits up in surprise, eyes widening as his mouth falls open. But he doesn't say anything at first. Then he sits back, pretends to relax and says: 'What brings this on? Who's been gossiping?'

'Ivy Rutt said I look like Flora Hammermeyer and I just wonder why I've never even heard of her, seeing she's my great-grandmother.'

'Trust old Ivy,' Dad mumbles. But he looks me in the eye now. 'Grandma Hammermeyer was never discussed much in the family,' he says, 'and I guess we shouldn't start now.'

'Was she already dead when you were young?'

'Not dead. Gone. That's all I know. And you don't look that much like her anyway.'

'Do you have a photo of her?'

'You are persistent, girl. I'd have to search. She may be in a group photo, but I doubt it. Now can I relax and read the paper?' He picks up The Platypus Argus and pretends to get absorbed in real estate ads. You'd think he was checking values to sell the farm. I know times are bad, but I hope that isn't on the cards.

So Flora Hammermeyer left. But Grandpa Arend was still alive here on Platypus when I was tiny, living in the room now occupied by Auntie Branka. His large, sad, sunburnt face always had a pipe stuck into it and the smoke made me cough. He was as quiet as a wallaby. Nothing like Auntie Branka, who gives her opinions on everything. I wonder, would she have known Flora Hammermeyer?

2: Auntie Branka's History of Platypus Island

Auntie Branka is one of Platypus Island's surviving local characters who have seen all the changes. 'First there were sealers, whalers and fishers,' she'd say. 'Then came the shooters, the men of the law and the lighthouse keepers. The keepers of the lights brought women and then there were kids. So far so good. We weren't too civilised yet. But then came the farmers with more women and children, followed by preachers who built churches on opposite corners in Queenscape. The other corners had pubs. Then followed shopkeepers and the agents of trading houses. Now the shooters are gone, the road is sealed and the animals protected, but the people ... well, they don't rely on each other any more like we used to when we were just a few large families.'

Auntie Branka was born on a farm, but spent her married life on a lighthouse cliff, where her only child, a boy, died of pneumonia. Her version of Platypus Island's history is the saga of one wave of people following another and how they pushed each other around or sideways.

'Take the councillors who now make all the decisions,' she'd say, 'or the graders and shearers who earn the quick money – they're all really farmers earning an extra buck on the side. The sportclubs and the choirs and the Island Women's Club and the Feisty Fiddlers are all stacked with sheep farmers and their wives, all complaining that times aren't what they used to be. But the lightkeepers, the fishers and the ferrymen never whinged, they faced danger every day. And the migrants, like our family and your Great-grandpa Arend, they never whinged. Teachers, nurses, doctors and builders came much later. But the best time was when the lighthouse keepers were the knights of our rugged coasts, rescuing people from shipwrecks. We all knew each other and we held wonderful parties at Christmas and the winter solstice.'

'Why didn't Aboriginal people ever settle here?' I asked, hoping she had an answer I hadn't found at school.

'Nobody knows. They had reasons of their own no doubt. Some say our island was regarded as the realm of the dead, but no mainland Aborigines ever confirmed that.'

I consider how weird it is to live in Australia without ever having gone to school with the first people of this country, about whose cultures we learned so much.

'What about the rangers?' I would ask to keep her going.

'Rangers? The older ones are recycled lighthouse keepers now that the lights are automatic,' she'd growl. 'We didn't have wildlife parks and bush reserves before you and Arend were born. They're a good thing, I grant you. But apart from rangers we now get researchers and scientists, because Platypus Island is so frightfully unique. And then, ever since unemployment started to bite on the mainland, we've been getting hippies and artists.'

'They're not the same though, are they?' I would nudge her.

'I grant you that. There's good potters and weavers and woodworkers and painters. And right there at the top are the literati, the people of the bookclub and those poets who gather in Queenscape. All to the good. A bit of culture never hurt anyone. Even the visiting lamas in their red robes bring something to the island that nobody else did: a place to retreat to for those who want that. We Slavs were always outsiders. We never built a church for ourselves in case that might have been frowned upon. But now there is a little temple at Return Rock and I think that's a good thing! Did you hear they call it Rebirth Rock? Those lamas have a sense of humour!'

'There aren't any hippies left on Platypus, are there?'

'Don't think so. Even hippies grow up. Plenty of hermits though. Headed by that layabout Tom Baudin. And now we have the yachties, the blow-ins with their airstrips, the young hopefuls buying up bankrupt farms, then splitting them up. And the visitors. Not to mention those dr-e-a-d-ful developers!'

However much I prodded, I could never get her to say a word about Tom Baudin. She clearly didn't think much good of him. I wondered whether they were boyfriend and girlfriend once, until I considered the age difference. Auntie Branka is at least fifteen years younger.

I tap on her door. She's Mum's only aunt and they are the last survivors of the Boudofski family that settled on Platypus in the 1880s. She is sitting up in bed, knitting and listening to the radio. She knits all our jumpers, socks and beanies.

'Would you like a hot drink, Auntie Bee?'

'Bianka, darling. A cup of cocoa with honey, please, my sweet.'

I make her cocoa in the kitchen, stirring it well, and return to sit in the creaking cane chair at the foot of her bed. Her hands move ceaselessly above a plum-coloured sleeve for Mum's new cardigan. Auntie Branka can barely move about with a walking frame and mostly uses her wheelchair, but her hands are as supple as mine. The radio program is about an exhibition of Japanese art. Auntie turns it off.

'Bianka darling, that was a lovely pudding you made. It had a different taste. What did you put in?'

'Cardamom and honey. Auntie Bee, I want to ask you something. Did you know my Great-grandma Flora Hammermeyer?'

Auntie Branka also startles at the name, dropping her knitting in her lap. 'Flora? Flora?! My goodness, yes! Who would not know Flora? The talk of the island. The beautiful, talented Flora, bent on per-fec-tion! The perfection of the mind, more so than the body or the house. All the energy your dear mother puts into the whole family, including me, Flora put into her own mind. All her waking hours she seemed to be really living somewhere else.'

I am shocked. That last bit sounds like me. Maybe I don't only look like Flora, but have a mind like hers. 'Did she read books, Auntie?'

'Ah, she was a very, ve-ry clever woman, always consulting the books. And wise in a whispy sort of way. Beautiful and talented. But she did not flourish here.' As Auntie Branka shakes her head, all her tight grey curls tremble.

'What sort of talents did she have, Auntie?'

'Her talents! They were of the mind. She was a thinker! She could think about anything and nothing, whether it had to do with the farm or the family, or what happened on Platypus or Kangaroo Island, or what happened in the world. She was always reading newspapers and books and she understood every-thing. She painted pictures too. And always she was writing in her diary in the evening, so I heard.'

Diary. She kept a diary like I do. 'Why did she leave, Auntie?'

'Leave? Aiai, she was so much older than me. And we Boudofskis lived on the east side and always spoke Russian or dialect. My English was not good then. So what could I understand of the problems of mar-ried couples? People talk. But I think – don't talk to anyone about this – I think she was too clever and wise and feeling unhappy about the life here. It was rough, you know. We hunted, killed and slaughtered to keep alive in those days. Platypus was twenty-five years behind Kangaroo Island.'

'Yeh, it still is and Kanga is twenty-five years behind the mainland. That means Platypus is half a century behind the mainland.' I nearly add: 'Even though we now have telephones, cars and computers.' But Auntie wouldn't be impressed.

'So it is, so it is. But sometimes that can be a good thing. People here keep each other honest. Hardly any crime. Now I must finish reading my book and then to sleep. Thank you for the nice pudding and the cocoa. You are becoming a very good cook, my darling.'

When Auntie Branka has talked more than she thinks she ought to, she always has to finish a book and go to sleep. I kiss her goodnight, collect my sketchbook from my room and sit at the table in the livingroom, where it is warm. All evening I sketch and rub out, until I have a pretty stylish picture of a girl in a button-up, two-piece adventure suit with a hood. There are pockets on the thighs, hips, chest and sleeves. I could make it from cut up old jeans turned inside out. There's a heap in the storeroom. And for buttons, I'll ask Dad to slice up a good mulga stick and drill the holes myself.

All evening I am possessed by thoughts of Great-gran Flora Hammermeyer and her diary, her beauty and her wisdom. Could I really be a little bit like her? There are only two generations between us. What sort of a flower was Flora? I draw a tall, elegant, frilly iris with slender leaves alongside the girl in the adventure suit. Then I clap the book shut and say goodnight. I want to do some deep thinking in privacy.

Soon I will have to share my room again. During the visitors season Coral and Zora move in with me. Yvan and the family computer share with Arend, who likes looking up farm prices and long-range weather forecasts on the internet. Then the two free rooms, opening onto the glassed-in verandah, become paying guest rooms in summer. But I can still enjoy my solitude for a few more months.

I love my room. If I left home I'd miss it terribly. I would have to take my log-cabin quilt, made by Mum before she got sick. And the white horse poster, the brass incense burner, my twenty books and my wallaby fur slippers.

One winter it rained so much that Dad could hardly do any work on the farm. He often gets new ideas when he is cooped up inside. So he went across to Kanga to buy cheesemaking supplies and a list of things for Mum's sewing. But he also brought back a dozen kangaroo and wallaby skins. He'd bought them from a woman who skinned animals killed on the roads and tanned the skins. She sold the meat as frozen petfood to a string of customers. But she also raised joeys if there were any alive in a dead mother's pouch, to return them to the wild later on.

It is a strange thing that the roads of Kanga are littered with dead kangaroos, wallabies and possums, whereas you hardly see any cadavers on Platypus Island. On the mainland they kill people on the roads. You see bouquets of flowers tied to trees with placards saying 'WE'LL NEVER FORGET YOU' and 'DIED TOO YOUNG', or a heart-shaped balloon with a name on it, or little white crosses stuck in the grass like you see in cemeteries. And the cars still speed past as if no one died there. Here on Platypus we have a speed limit of 50 kilometres, so you can brake in time if humans or animals crossing the road become transfixed by your headlights. Only visitors break the limit sometimes. Fast-track people.

Dad said the Kanga woman did a wonderful job, raising scores of joeys in old socks hanging from the knobs of kitchen chairs, feeding them a special formula with vitamins, taking them to bed at night to keep them warm. Dad says she has a right to the skins and meat of the killed animals and provides a service by removing them.

She told him her worst nightmares came true when she found a dead animal she'd once raised herself and set free. She can tell them all apart. She gave that one a burial. In the visitors season she admits people to her enclosure with young animals for a fee, shows them the joeys in socks and the feeding area behind the kitchen. She hands cards to visitors with a picture of a wallaby sitting by the roadside, staring at the body of his dead mate. On the back it says:

My beloved lies so still
I fear she'll bounce no more
With me through bush and dale.
My heart feels awful sore.'

And underneath:

'Please do not exceed 50k.
Give the animals a chance.
This is their land.

I wish I could work for someone like that. I feel admiration for what she is doing. That winter Dad measured our feet and made skin slippers with the fur turned inside and we've never had cold feet since. He makes new ones for Arend and me as we grow and the littlies get our hand-me-downs, because they hardly wear out.

From the woman who rescues joeys from dead mothers' pouches, skins road kills, delivers pet meat on her rounds and educates locals and visitors, my thoughts turn to Flora Hammermeyer who may have left because life on Platypus was all killing and butchering. If that woman and Flora had lived at the same time, would they have understood that they each loved nature in their own way, or would Flora have turned away from her because of the skinning and petfood business? But how can it be avoided?

People eat meat, but they let someone else do the

killing and dissecting. We eat farm-killed meat, from our own or another farm. Dad and Arend do it if they have to. I wouldn't mind going vegetarian, but that's difficult at home. Dad wouldn't understand, Mum would worry I wasn't getting enough 'goodness', Arend would rubbish me. Of course I could just cut less and less meat for myself, pretending to be not hungry.

Whenever I see sheep and cattle grazing as if they're having a peaceful life, I think of how they eventually end up on dinner plates. Lambs doing crazy jumps in springtime remind me of a butcher's window in Queenscape: 'Spring lamb this Xmas'. Painted on the window are lambs in green grass strewn with flower petals, an angel above them. And a mother saying to her little girl: 'See the little lammies on the window?' But the lammies lie in the window, sliced up into little pink chops. Oh my unknown Great-gran Flora! You and I must be very much alike in our heart of hearts. What happened to you? Where did you escape to?

Sitting up in bed in my nightie, wrapped in my quilt, diary open on a blank page, I cannot make sense of these emotions fighting inside me. Only one thing becomes certain. I must find out more about Flora Hammermeyer. Her life could be the key to my future. If I can understand what moved her, I may have some idea what sort of adult I am going to be.

Suddenly, an idea. In Mum and Dad's room is the wooden box where photo albums are kept. Sneak in now, take some old albums and put them back tomorrow.

Platypus slippers are soundless. Shining my torch into their bedroom, I try to lift the brass clip that holds down the lid of the box. It is stiff, but with a bit of wrenching it flips up. I shine the torch inside and recognise the floral plastic covers of the latest albums. Pushing them up with one hand, I spot a brown cardboard book and a grey one near the bottom. I think I saw these years ago, but I wasn't looking for Great-gran Flora then. I lift them out and the others sag back. Shutting the lid, I put back the lace cover cloth and glide back to my room.

One album goes under the blankets. I take a large book from my shelf, *Seashells of the Southern Oceans*. Opening it midway, I place the other album inside and sit both up on my knee. Just in case someone comes in for a late night chat. In a house full of people you have to protect your privacy at all times. Who wants to answer embarrassing questions.

Scanning the little brown snapshots of the Woodsman family and their friends, I discover Dad as a six-year-old with knobbly knees. A family picnic on the beach. The old man is with them, pipe stuck in his face. Flora must have been gone already. Maybe she is in the other album. I quickly change the grey one for the brown one. Opening the cover, I doubt now I've ever seen this album before. A musty smell of years gone by rises from thick charcoal-coloured pages. Some photos hang half out of the yellowed photo corners that fix them on the page.

There's a young man on the cliff with a pipe in his mouth. Can it be Great-grandpa Arend? Here he is again, with a woman. A beautiful woman. I peer at the sepia print for detail. I can just make out my own arched eyebrows, my straight nose, my high cheekbones. She wears a long flowing summer gown with ribbons and looks like a just-opened frilly iris. Her smile was just lighting up when the photo was taken. Or maybe it was beginning to fade because the shutterbug was slow. Behind her the waves carry little white heads and her long hair is blown sideways by the wind.

I turn the page. A photo of a woman's back, hair in a loose bun, a baby peering over her shoulder. Then two little kids on a sheepskin, a boy sitting up and a girl lying down on her tum. Unmistakably Grandma Barb's round little face. So these were Flora's children and that boy left and never returned. Again I recognise my eyebrows, nose and cheekbones. He has my face as well! Two faces just like mine and those two left the island and died somewhere else. Why?

Am I fated to do likewise? Or will I become island-bound? But I love Platypus, my island, and love does not bind. That's one of Auntie Branka sayings. I would rather live on an even smaller rock than go to Kanga or the mainland, as long as I could eke out a living somehow.

If no one in this family can or wants to tell me anything more about Flora and her son who went away, I will definitely visit Tom Baudin. Can't tomorrow, washing day. Wednesday we do the supply run, then mending and ironing. Can't let Mum down. But on Thursday she goes quilting all day, dropping Auntie Branka at the spinners club on the way. So, no baking day. I hope the weather is dry, because it's a slippery slope to climb to Tom's lookout.

Sleep won't come for a long time. I hear Mum and Dad go to their room, their muted voices. Yvan gets up to go to the toilet. I always know it's him because he hums to himself in the dark to keep spooks at bay. Sometimes he sits till late at the computer, chatting to internet friends anywhere in the world. Arend and I didn't have that when we were at school. Auntie Branka coughs her dry little cough. Beds creak and the wind tugs at the windows. Dreadlocks barks once, then paces the verandah, growling. Perhaps a wild animal is crossing the lawn, the garden is surrounded by thick scrub. Finally there is only a sliver of moon and the distant boom of waves crashing against the cliffs.

Suddenly I wake up from a dream, even though I thought I was still awake. In the dream three people come skipping arm in arm towards me, their hair flowing on the breeze. They are laughing and singing a one-line song. I cannot hear the words because of the wind. They stop not far away and look intently at me. The young man is handsome and dressed like a sailor in wide pants and tunic. The woman holds something in her outstretched hands. It looks like a small album, less than half the size of those under my blankets. Just as I am about to accept the album from her hands I look at the third person. With a shock I recognise my own face. I wake up with empty hands.

3: Panic on the Hoof

Late afternoon and raining. Dad and Arend come home early. Mum and I are still mending and ironing. Just as I'm about to walk into Mum and Dad's bedroom with an armful of folded bedlinen and Dad's good ironed shirts on hangers in the other hand, Dad comes out of that door with a face like thunder. With a pang of guilt I remember not having put the photo albums back. There just hasn't been an opportunity. But surely, he wouldn't know about that. I stack sheets and pillowcases in the old walnut wardrobe and hang the shirts on a rod behind the dark-red curtain with the lily pattern.

There's the evening meal to prepare. I stand at the cuttingboard in the kitchen corner of the living-room with my back to the family. Dad is rummaging through drawers in the china cabinet. Cleaving an onion, I think again of Flora. The halves are like a dancer's white pompom gowns. Chop-chop-chop and they become moon slivers. Did she dance when she was happy? She looked happy in the photo. Keeping busy, I feel a storm gathering behind my back. Some days! In a family of eight there's always something brewing.

'I've looked everywhere for the old family photo album,' Dad says in an accusing voice, 'and it's nowhere to be found. It ought to be in the box in the bedroom, but it isn't and I've turned over every other drawer in the house.'

There is a nonplussed silence. Mum mumbles about looking again in the box because it has to be there.

'I have looked three times,' Dad harps back. I feel his eyes boring between my shoulderblades. 'Bianka, could it be that you have the old album?'

Turning around slowly I show a blank face. 'What, Dad? An album?'

'Yes. You asked me for a photo, didn't you?'

'Oh yes,' I say. Then suddenly I feel nauseous for pretending I do not know what he means and blurt out: 'Yes, I found it myself. I looked in an old photo album. It's in my room. I'll put it back.' I turn again to the chopping board and attack the carrots.

'And may I ask who gave you permission to go into our room and take that album out of our box?' Dad thunders. He's as mad as a snake.

I'm turning cold. Putting down the knife I swing around to confront him and am struck to see his face contorted in anger. You'd think I'd committed a major crime, soiling his good name for all time. Anger rises inside me too. Why can't I see the family photos? Words begin tearing out of me in a tumult.

'Dad, you are being very unfair. You didn't say you would look for the photo. Remember, I came to you first, but you showed no interest whatsoever. I did nothing wrong. I simply took two albums to look at old photos. Everybody knows they're in that wooden box. That's no secret, is it? And I am a member of this family, aren't I? If I can walk in and out of your room with the washing and your shirts that I ironed, why can't I walk in there to borrow a family photo album? Please tell me why!'

I am spouting white fire now and my whole body trembles. Arend and Mum stare at me and the littlies stand stunned in the doorway. Dad's face has gone pale, but he still holds a pose as if he would like to hit something.

Finally – it's only seconds – he sits down in his armchair and pushes the hair from his forehead. 'Bianka,' he says in a strangled voice, 'of course you have a right to walk into any room in this house – as your birthright and as a member of this family. If only you'd told me or Mum that you'd borrowed the album.'

All the fire in me dies down. 'I'm sorry, Dad. Next time I'll tell you.' I turn and chop the carrots as the tears start rolling. I turn on the oven to heat the quiche I've made in between everything else and generally make myself scarce and busy. I feel as if I have bruised myself. Behind my back family life resumes. Normality returns noisily. But something has changed. Dad has just acknowledged that I am an adult member of this household. A child no longer. But there's also a sense of loss. Have I lost Dad's trust?

It irks me now that I acted like a child by sneaking into their room to get the albums and then hid them. I could simply have said I was going to look up some photos and would put them back and they would probably have said: go ahead. Since I am becoming an adult I'd better start acting like one. No more secret business. Secrets cause too many hassles.

As soon as this thought is born, I realise I cannot tell anyone I'm going to see Tom Baudin tomorrow. Dad is not over-friendly with Tom, although I don't know why. He was not pleased when I did the oral history project on Tom. It's not that he ever says anything against the old hermit, but time and again Mum and Dad hammer into us that we must not go anywhere alone without permission. And since the latest outbursts of terrorism seem to move closer, Dad sometimes gets paranoid, even though we live at the very end of the world.

I know there is one good reason. Half the year our island's population swells with visitors from the mainland. Most are nice people on holiday, but occasionally somebody causes trouble. One year there was a spate of robberies, mostly old things that lie around people's verandahs and sheds until they want to use them. The Platypus police caught one guy red-handed as he carried off Shaun Marshland's mum's heritage porcelain flowerpots, just as Shaun came up the driveway. There turned out to be a gang stealing portable antiques to sell on the mainland. 'For drugs,' said Auntie Branka, always better informed than any of us.

But the one that drove the fear of hell into all parents came two springs ago. I never saw the man. They say he was slick and cool and the girls of Queenscape hung around him like flies around a honey pot. He must have been handsome and a smooth talker, because several girls 'went too far', so the gossip went. And now the fellow has three babies on Platypus, all roughly the same age. But the father was never seen again. We Platypus girls were just about put in chains from mid-season on. Understandable I suppose, but I would have liked at least the satisfaction of resisting the guy's now legendary charms.

Mum and Dad would still let me ride Whoopsy or go walking with Stephen, my romantic friend, because we've been bush and beach walking since we were kids. And how could they stop it and not offend his paying guest parents? But last summer I received veiled warnings from Dad to 'walk and talk but play no other games', while Mum looked more worried than usual.

You wonder what parents think when they come out with such brain twisters. Why don't they call a spade a spade? Do they really think you can grow up to be nearly eighteen and not know what happens between men and women? Don't they know we get sex education at school? We have learned how to protect ourselves. That does not mean you're going to go all the way. Although, three Queenscape girls did. I heard they are firm friends now, having set up house together so their children will be real brother and sisters. They babysit for each other and take part-time jobs. I admire that. People at first looked down on them for being 'fallen women'. Island people can act not a little superior sometimes, as if this was a brand new sin. But the girls are thinking of how best to bring up their kids.

So Stephen and I walked and talked, sometimes holding hands. Usually we'd go for a swim. I always wore my swimsuit under my clothes. Never had any problems with Stephen. Some girls tempt the boys, but I don't. Maybe I'm a late developer. That would be right! But it would be a shame to spoil the friendship I have with Stephen by getting into a lot of necking and the rest. I know from the girls at school that after that starts there's no walking and talking any more. All the guys do from then on is chase around the island in their cars, like wound-up toys, looking for places to be alone with a girl. Secret business again. I'm trying to get away from that. I want to be liked for my walking, talking self, before thinking of love. Seriously!

At the table I cut panels from a pile of old jeans. Told Mum what I wanted to make and she said: 'You're welcome to them. People give me so many to cut down for the littlies, I could dress an orphanage if I had the energy.'

She hasn't the energy she used to have, poor Mum. Radiotherapy after the operation tired her out completely. So I get up and make the evening coffee and bring Auntie Branka her cocoa. She's listening to the radio, nodding her head in agreement. 'All politicians are fibbers,' she says to no one in particular. 'The country survives in spite of 'em, but they claim the glory and pretend to speak for us all!'

'Do you want to come into the livingroom, Auntie Bee?' I ask. 'We're just sitting around doing our own things.'

'Ai, no! The radio is too interesting tonight. And I'm going to finish my book.'

I kiss her goodnight and smell eau-de-cologne. She makes a lot of sense, my Auntie Branka. Must ask her one day about Tom Baudin when he was younger. Seeing that even her mum was born on Platypus, I haven't asked enough questions about the past. But that is about to change.

∽

In the morning I run out in my nightie to be struck dumb by the beauty of a new day. The sun is not up yet and it is chilly, but the sky runs to colours of opal and the birds sing at the top of their little lungs. In the distance the waves crash onto the cliffs and the air is thin and fresh, without any smells yet, so that you feel something is about to happen. A surge of love for my island takes hold of me. With hands folded across my chest because of the snappy cold, I contain my excitement. I love Platypus! What luck to be born an islander!

To avoid freezing into a statue, I run to the vegetable garden and pick chives, mustard and lettuce leaves to put in Dad's sandwiches of homemade sheep cheese and pickles. He is off early to Queenscape for a land deal. I didn't think we were that financial, but Arend whispered that Auntie Branka is putting up money for Mum and Dad to buy the wedge-shaped strip of land between our farm and the ocean. It has just been put up for sale by the mainland owner, who planned to build a holiday shack but never did. If it becomes ours, we have a clear run to the beach and the cliffs. I know Dad always wanted to protect a bit of coast from humans and let the seals live there in peace, but coasts belong to everyone.

When I hand Dad his lunch pack he gives me a quick left-handed hug. 'My girl,' he says and is out the door. So we're friends again. Tears prick behind my eyelids. All that emotion yesterday and now this. I pull myself together under a hot shower.

Arend has already milked our few milking sheep and goes off fishing. He always brings enough for a meal, so we do chips and salad tonight. He trots off on Whoopsy, our old mare, with Dreadlocks at her hooves. That means I have no choice but to walk to Tom Baudin's cabin. I put celery sticks and apples into the littlies lunchboxes, then chuck half a handful of almonds and raisins in twists of paper. We never get money to buy snacks at school because we can't afford it, but I try to put more variety in their lunches than Arend and I had.

By half past nine Mum and Auntie Branka set off in the car for their craft day. It's nice to have the farm all to myself. As soon as they are gone I peel potatoes, wrap them in wet teatowels and put them in a dish in the fridge, ready for chipping tonight. It's time I stop thinking of Coral as one of the littlies – she's just turned fifteen. She should help with the cooking, since she always talks about food. Tonight she can fry chips, while I toss the salad.

The sound of a horse's hooves coming nearer. Arend already? But why would he come up the driveway if he took off in the direction of the sea? Quickly I draw the thin curtain across the window to look out without being seen. Although it's broad daylight, it suddenly feels spooky to be alone on the farm. The sound of a galloping horse grows steadily louder.

The very moment horse and rider round the bushes that hide the bend, I duck away from the window, slide on my socks through the passage and step into the broom closet. I wrench the key out of the lock and turn it from the inside. That horrible Patrick Byderdike! That rat! He must have nearly collided with Mum's car at the top of the driveway and he would know everyone else is out working. What is he after? Who is he after?

I wait. Is there enough air in here to survive? For how long? I hear knocking and his voice. Then the outer door is opened and he shouts: 'Anybody home?' He jolly well knows nobody but me could be home at this time of day. I'm trapped like a rabbit in a hole.

'Anybody about? Hello there!' I can hear him walk around the kitchen. The potato peelings and the knife are still lying on the board. It's obvious I just ran out. How far is that wretch prepared to go? He's pestered me often enough at barn dances and the animal fair, until I've stopped going. Nothing serious I suppose, but I always felt disturbed by his pushy attentions and snake-like eyes. He's older than most guys that hang out at dances because he isn't married, never even had a girlfriend. No wonder. What is the jackal doing in our kitchen?

Finally I hear the door being pulled shut and foot-steps on the verandah. Phew! He's going. But no! He is walking around the house, making the verandah boards by the bedrooms creak. The nerve! What if I lay sick in bed with the flu and that creep turned up at the window, looking in? Can I ever find privacy anywhere in this world? Now he's walking back the way he came. Then the horse whinnies. He's finally going. I hear the hooves clip-clopping, removing that despicable character.

I'm not game to come out yet, in case he's trying to trick me. What can I do to stop this guy bothering me? Tell Dad? Or Arend? I listen to the deadly silence outside the closet. The horse has gone. Could he crawl back soundlessly? If he did, he would have to come up the driveway again. Maybe I'd better get out of the house quick smart via the rear and hide in the scrub.

I turn the lock. It sqeaks. I wait. No sound. I open the door and step into the passage. The house feels empty. I'd know if someone was breathing under the same roof as me. I sneak back into the kitchen, put the peelings in the compost bucket, put away the knife. Into my shoes, grab my jacket, hat and pack. Wrap the sandwiches I'd put aside for myself, pick up two apples. Water bottle, quick.

I lock the outer door on the inside and sneak back through the passage and out through the laundry. Lock that door and slide the key under a rock. I'll be back before anyone else comes home, but just in case I don't, they know where to find it. I run into the scrub and come to a standstill to let my pounding heart calm down. My ears seem to have grown into giant shells. I hear a thousand sounds as I try to figure out whether I am alone or have unwanted company. But all the sounds come from birds and insects, the wind and the ocean, leaves on the trees and a distant cow. My heartbeat returns to normal. I am alone on the farm. A few deep sighs release the tension.

Now I must figure out a way to Tom Baudin's cabin without crossing any horse trails. The quickest way is to follow our fence line and take the risk to cross the neighbour's paddock. Shaun's brother Dereck farms two properties and lives at the other, so it would be unlucky if he was there. Even then, I suppose he wouldn't mind me taking a shortcut.

Keeping to the scrub line I set a brisk pace. Walking is a relief. I now begin to sense tension throughout my body, as if I'd been attacked or assaulted. How to explain to anyone that I hid in the broom closet because someone came to the door? How to explain that Patrick Byderdike seriously bothers me? I have no proof. He never said anything that I could quote to state my case. Nor has he actually stalked me or asked me to go out with him. People might think I am making this up. And yet, when he is within sight I stiffen with … with what? Fear? No, not just that.

Soft sand slows me down. Here the land, so close to the beach, is useless for farming. Lots of wildflowers are out and bees buzz about gathering nectar. Arend's hives collect enough honey to sell a handsome surplus. Platypus Island honey is famous. Already the scent of honey is on the air, although it's only spring. At the end of the scrub I have to run across open paddock for half a kilometre to reach the next shelterbelt. No trails here, yet I stop and peer in all directions. But the horizons are free of moving horsemen. I run for it, my pack bobbing on my back.

I'm beginning to enjoy the day that began so beautiful. A blue wren and its plain-looking mate fly up from the first flowering shrubs when I reach them.

Honeyeaters skate on the air in flocks of half a dozen and in the paddock plovers stand about holding a staff meeting. Tom Baudin's cliff is visible from here. Lucky the sun is out – the trail may be dry. Don't know how he manages to drive his old truck up there, let alone coming down!

It's getting warm and I catch a whiff of my own sweat. A quick gulp of water and I take off my jacket, tying the sleeves around my waist. Suddenly it hits me. Patrick Byderdike is a prowler! A sort of terrorist, really. Even when he walks up to you in public, he prowls. And I have proof for it, because what business did he have going around the verandah looking into all the bedroom windows?

I'll tell Arend tonight and he can speak to Dad and maybe they will just spill a word or two when they meet other island men, so that word gets around that Patrick Byderdike is a prowler. Maybe then he'll leave me alone. It's a relief having found the right word to describe my feelings. Amazing what support one single definition can be when you're in trouble.

Two glossy black cockatoos fly up from a copse of casuarinas, disturbed in their feasting on seed cones. The brilliant scarlet of their tail feathers flashes in the sunlight. These birds are now utterly rare. It is a good omen seeing them fly across my path. On some days magic is in the air. I can do with a touch of magic today.

4: Tom the Hermit and my Great-Grandma

As the shelterbelt peters out, Tom's cliff rises before me. I crawl under a wire fence to walk around the cliff base along a muddy trail, Tom's path to the cove where he does his fishing. Coming to the bottom of the track I spot his truck up there. I begin the climb, making sure to place my feet on something firm. My fabulous new sneakers grip the rocks and hoist me up. Dad paid a packet for them; he said I deserved them for helping out at home. He notices more than we realise.

At the top my heart pounds again, not wildly like an hour ago, but strong and steady after the climb. Not too loudly I call: 'Cooee! Are you there, Mr. Baudin? It's Bianka.' I walk to the door and knock, not too hard in case he's having a nap and wakes up with a start. But chair legs scrape the wooden floor and Tom's slow steps approach the door. He opens it wide and stands old and bent in his grey shirt and trousers, his hair white, his eyes grey as the morning sky. He smiles his lopsided smile.

'I was thinking only the other day that I haven't seen Bianka for a long time,' he says. For a hermit he speaks long sentences. Obviously I'm not disturbing him. 'Come in, lass,' he says and I do.

I love Tom's cabin. Everything in it is useful. Apart

from the table, two chairs, a bed and a stove, there are hooks on the walls holding tools, rods, nets, clothes and hats. By the stove two cooking pots. And above his bed a tiny shelf holding seven old books with faded spines. I don't dare ask whether I may look at the titles. Which seven books would I take if I went to live a hermit's life on my secret Sometime Island? He has a crackling old radio. The cabin smells of fish, salt and kerosene.

'Will you have a cup of tea?' asks Tom, not waiting for my nod. 'And how is your father nowadays? And your good mother?' He's forgotten that Mum has been ill and in hospital, if he ever knew. So I say: 'They are well, and pretty busy.'

'Ah, busy. Everyone is busy these days. Are you getting busy too, or will you escape the rat race?' He looks at me intently. I escaped one rat this morning and raced to do so. Tom fills a kettle by dipping a cup into a waterbucket. He lights the kerosene primus and rinses two cups in a bowl on the table, carefully wiping them with a grey teatowel.

'I haven't joined the rat race yet,' I answer. 'I'm helping Mum at home. But I'll have to do something about my future soon. I may apply to Parks & Wildlife.' I only say this to say something, because I'm even less decided what to do now that I am on the trail of the talented Flora.

Tom seems to think for a moment. Then he says: 'Well, that may suit you very well. But they are part of the bureaucracy, you know. Some of those rangers are little bureaucrats building their little empires. They are employing more young girls to please the public, but how possible is it for the girls to get ahead in a male domain?'

What a modern thought for such an ancient man. Tom talks like Auntie Branka, but more learned. I let his words sink in. 'I understand what you're saying,' I answer. But actually, his words rock me. Is there no place in the world where a girl can live, work and be happy? 'Maybe girls will change Parks & Wildlife when everyone gets used to them being there,' I add weakly.

Tom looks pensively out to sea. From his crusty window panes you see nothing but the horizon and the ocean reaching all the way to Antarctica. 'The older I get,' he says, 'the more despondent I become about human society's capacity for change. Yet, change is nature's main pursuit. But it is the likes of you that keep old hopes alive. You are a very bright girl, Bianka, and I hope the island will never lose you to the world.'

He doesn't think much of the world, that's why he is a hermit. This may be the right moment to pop my question. 'Mr. Baudin, when you first came to Platypus did you know my great-grandmother, Flora Hammermeyer?'

Tom's gaze switches from the sea to my face and his grey eyes suddenly turn black. They are clouded darkly with an emotion I do not understand and for the second time today I am frightened, though not of the old man.

The kettle starts singing a faint melody that gathers strength as the water nears boiling point. Tom still sits nailed to his chair, looking out to sea again. He has not spoken a word since my fatal question. Finally he gets up to answer the kettle's call. I don't dare to move, frightened to break the spell that has taken hold of him. How to know whether it is fury or grief that fills him to bursting point? I would rather escape now, but don't dare do that either as I would forever lose the chance to hear what he knows.

Tom drops tea leaves into the boiling water, adds two tablespoons of sugar and a long squirt of tinned milk, and stirs. The hermit's way of making tea. He stirs vigorously. Thick, milky liquid pours from the spout into the cups. Not until he sits down again does Tom turn to me.

'Flora, the goddess of flowers. You have inherited her features,' he says unexpectedly. I startle. How well did he know her then?

'Yes,' I quaver. 'And her son's face too.'

Again Tom turns his eyes away before he speaks again.

'The handsome, talented Frederik. Frederik with a "k", the Scandinavian way. A boy of so much promise, who had to leave these islands because of a fistful of gossiping vipers.'

'Did he also live on Kangaroo Island then before he disappeared?'

'He tried, until the slime followed him. But he did not disappear. He only disguised his tracks for the unworthy few. Those that love him know where to reach him.'

'Is he alive?' I ask in amazement. Nothing goes as expected today. I came to discover Flora and am handed ... what is he to me? 'Is he my ...?'

'Being your great-grandmother's son, I'd guess that makes him your great-uncle. Yes, he is alive and quite well, possessing the genes of survival inherited from his father. And the town where he lives has become a better place for his settling there.'

'Gosh!' I want to ask many questions, but hope Tom's flow continues unprodded.

'He is as talented as his mother. He always possessed a creative energy, a talent for organising, and a way to win people. His mother was good at whatever she turned her hand at: gardening, painting, writing, needlework ... and she sang like a lark. It was Flora who established the first native garden on Platypus with plants, rocks and shells from the bush and a sight to behold it was. Then she painted pictures of a hundred local species and wrote their descriptions. Afterwards ... after her departure, Frederik had the book published and he uses it still in his teaching. He set up a wonderful school for the environment, long before anyone thought of it. He trained the first environmental scientists Australia ever had. Even in his old age … oh well, he'll never catch up with me of course …' Tom chuckles and the darkness leaves his eyes. 'Even now he travels widely to give talks and advise on land, forest, river and coastal restoration.'

Tom sits back to slurp his tea. How does he know so much about Flora's son? Are they keeping in touch?

'Did he and Flora leave together?' I ask.

'He left after the war, just thirteen, for an education on the mainland. Flora visited him several times a year. He went on to teachers' college and gained honours, but he only came back twice, hoping to teach on Kanga to be near her. But as I mentioned before, the slime of gossip followed him there and he went where no one knew him and he would be judged on his own merits.'

'What were the islanders judging him for then?'

'Not all the islanders. Just a handful, but a few can poison anyone's life.' Just one can do that, I thought.

'There are people who have extraordinary amounts of uncontrolled energy. It has to go somewhere or they will self-destruct. So they aim it at other people, for whatever reason they can easily pick up on. It doesn't really matter what as far as they're concerned. Of course, some self-destruct in that process, because sometimes the victims of their bile hit back. There were some nasty incidents on Kanga in the early days – that's a long time ago now. The islands had wild beginnings, child. You wouldn't want to know about it.'

'The sealers,' I say. 'We learned about them at school.'

'Sanitised, no doubt!' snorts Tom. 'They don't ever tell you what really took place, so as not to spoil the glorious story of settlement.'

'No, truly Mr. Baudin, we got the bad parts of the story of settlement too,' I defend my teachers. 'I know they were rough and there were human tragedies and I wonder is that why Flora left Platypus Island?'

An invisible curtain seems to slide across Tom's face again. He pours more tea in our cups. Then he turns to me, asking: 'Bianka, how old are you now?'

'Almost eighteen.'

'Almost a grown-up young woman. Almost the age at which Flora married Hammermeyer. Perhaps I should tell you what really happened. But your parents may blame me for it, so you'd better keep it to yourself.'

I nod, frightened to speak and break his train of thought.

'She was the granddaughter of an artist-convict who'd been sent to Tasmania for his political views, which did not coincide with those of the establishment that ruled England and its colonies. Eventually he got his ticket of leave for good behaviour, but he was so starved of gentle company that he fell in love with the first girl that looked after him, the maid of a Hobart boarding house. She was a currency lass, a born islander and as smart as she was generous. So they were happy and produced one daughter who married a trader and Flora was their only grandchild. The last time the family gathered was at Flora's wedding to Arend Hammermeyer, who'd walked off a ship trading in the coastal settlements.'

Tom's voice croaks. He stops to stare out to sea, where he seems to find his balance. He's unused to so much talking. So Flora was an island woman after all.

'Whether she loved him or not is neither here nor there. She was young and impressionable and he a strapping trader with an exotic accent. He took her to the mainland and when South Australia went into drought he came looking for cheap land. They came to Kangaroo Island on a trading boat, but one land deal fell through and he pushed on to Platypus. He bought up half the island. Perhaps I exaggerate, maybe it was a quarter. I guess your family knows how big his holdings were, but bit by bit he sold it all off, not always at the best price. He sold out to give Flora what she wanted, a fine big house with high ceilings and a studio to paint in. It still stands at Sundew Cove, dilapidated by now, no doubt. Only the gods know how they got building materials, furniture and especially her piano over those saddle hills before the road came through.'

'I know that house,' I say in surprise, but miffed that no one ever told me it was built for Flora. 'It still is the only house at Sundew Cove. My friend Sylvie lives there and I sometimes stay over with her. Only the studio is in bad repair, but Sylvie's brothers are going to restore it for guests.'

Tom snorts again. 'She did her best paintings there. If I hadn't been who I was, I could have bought the place from Hammermeyer after she ... departed. I made good money in those days.'

'Did he not want to sell the place to you then?'

'Not over his dead body. You see, Bianka ... you are old enough to understand these things, I'm sure ... he would rather have sold me a knife to cut my own throat, than sell me the temple he built for Flora. Because when I came to Platypus, not long after they bought the land here, Flora and I fell in love.'

I gasp. 'Really?' Stupid thing to say, but what else ... How embarrassing and weird to hear a man in his eighties confess to me that he was in love with my great-grandmother.

'Yes. We took one look at each other at the post office on mail day and that was it. She had just turned twenty and I was all of nineteen. We met secretly and talked of eloping, but she gave up that idea when she found she was with child. She knew it was ours, but Arend Hammermeyer thought of course it was his and surrounded her with all the comforts money could buy. She didn't dare tell him, nor did she feel up to eloping with me, so she settled down to have the child that was Frederik.'

I am stunned. Flora's son was … is Tom's son. And if he is my great-uncle then I am also related to Tom!

'So you see, lassie, you and I are family, although officially we may not claim it.'

'Oh how awful. How could she keep pretending? She must have been so unhappy.'

'You understand her, lassie. One woman understands another across the abyss of time. Well, I remained her loyal friend, but there were few opportunities to show it. And then she had Barbara, your grandma, and remained a model wife and mother. But five years after World War Two ended, a wicked character filled her sherry glass just once too often at a party of the island squattocracy.'

Tom's voice breaks again and he is obviously angry, half a century after the event. 'She spilled the beans!' he says in a gravelly voice. 'And the island was not big enough for Arend Hammermeyer's fury and the gossip of those evil people, who had hinted all along that Frederik was my son. So eventually she packed up and left.'

'Did she never come back to Platypus?'

'Yes, once. But I can't tell you about that today. My voice is giving up.'

His voice has become a rasping of air. He is a very old man and he is sad and upset. I feel terribly burdened by his story, which is much more than I bargained for.

'May I come back another day, Mr. Baudin?' I

wonder even more now what his real name is. Why did he choose to wear another man's name? 'I can't often get away, but I'd like to …'

'You come, lassie. Any time.' His voice is recovering its strident tone.

'I brought you some homemade bread and apples from our tree.' I place the food on the table and he brightens. I have no appetite myself.

'That's good of you, lassie. You are as thoughtful as she was. Now take care on the way down, take the stick that stands by the door. It has a nail in it to get a grip on the track. Leave it in the bush at the bottom, for the next visitor.' He chuckles. 'Not many come these days. People are too busy.'

I quietly leave the cabin, shut the door, pick up the stick and make my way down to earth. Now I understand why he has become a hermit. And why Dad claims the family didn't discuss Flora Hammermeyer much. And why Great-grandpa Arend sat silently with a pipe stuck in his face for all those years thereafter.

Walking fast to Dereck's fence, I think of how people would have judged what Flora did. It would have been regarded as a terrible sin. No different today, really. Yet, Tom's grief and emotion tell me he and Flora were deeply in love, perhaps even meant for each other. Women were often married off for their own security in those wild days, and Arend must have looked a dependable son-in-law to her doting parents. Tom said she never saw her father and mother again.

They must have died. People didn't become very old in those days. And why did she return to Platypus? Did she live with the family again, or with Tom?

Oh, how terribly complex real love must be when it strikes. How can you ever be sure your first love is your only love? Could your first love really be the greatest and the last? From what you hear around, people do not know the answer and make plenty of mistakes. So did Flora. Perhaps not by falling in love with Tom, but by marrying Arend whom she hardly knew. But then, she didn't know Tom either. So what is the test of real love?

I am disturbed in my favourite pastime of thinking through life's mysteries by the ominous sound of horse's hooves on the trail leading up from the beach. I dive into Dereck's shelterbelt and hold my breath. Through the leaves I see Patrick Byderdike gallop up on his horse. Is he still riding around the island getting rid of his energy? I remember Tom's remark and am glad the wretch can't have seen me. But why is he prowling down at that beach, on the other side of Tom's cliff? He carries no baitbag or rod. He seems as footloose as he was this morning. His very appearance makes shivers run up and down my spine.

As the sound of hooves disappear in the direction of the bitumen, I run through the trees, through the paddock, into the scrub. There I take a breather and surprise a wallaby just passing through. It looks at me with its brown eyes until it decides I'm a statue and continues on its way, hopping in and out of the bushes. It is mid afternoon when I get home. Fetching the key from under the rock I let myself in. The house is empty. That feels good. The family will soon start arriving and they won't have a clue where I have been. Nor can I tell them.

Yesterday I resolved to have no secret business any more. Today I have been living through one intrigue after another. What is life doing to me? Or am I bringing this on myself in my quest to find out what sort of a person Flora was?

5: Role Models, Who Needs One!

Arend sidles up to me after I give him the secret sign that I need to talk to him. In a big family you develop ways and means. Except for Auntie Branka, everyone is in the kitchen-livingroom.

Standing side by side at the sink, Arend washes the fish he caught today and I cut chips. Out of the side of my mouth I tell him: 'I was home alone this morning when Patrick Byderdike galloped up on his horse. I hid in a closet, but he came into the kitchen and called 'anybody home?', and then he sneaked all around the verandah. He must have looked in every bedroom window.'

Arend is quick on the uptake. He knows all the island fellas. 'Has he ever bothered you?' he whispers.

'Not directly, but he used to prowl up to me at dances and at the fair and today he prowled around the house. He must have seen Mum and Auntie go out the driveway. Can you talk to Dad?'

'Can do,' Arend says and turns around with his bowl of fishes. 'Dad,' he calls across the room, 'Sorry to get you out of your chair, but I could do with a hand at the barbecue.' Dad, ever helpful, gets up without a murmur to follow Arend outside.

I turn my attention to Coral. 'Come here, big sis,' I say, 'I need you to look after the chips while I run for a salad.'

She's willing enough. That's one difference between our family and Sylvie's. Here you can usually count on co-operation. In Sylvie's family everyone passes the buck and jobs get endlessly postponed. Coral nods as I explain the principle of heating the oil, scorching the chips so they won't get soggy, then turning the flame low for cooking while tossing.

'The oven is on low, so you spread the ones that are ready on trays to keep warm, okay? You need to do them in four batches. You're a good kid!'

'Don't kid me,' shrugs Coral, shoves me aside, dons the apron and takes charge as if she were a pro. One day she just might be, too.

Running out with a bowl I pick radishes, endive, brown and green lettuce, sorrel, dandelion leaves, chives, and marigold flowers growing rampant between the vegetables. I'll whip up a quick dressing of yoghurt, lemon and mustard. Walking back to the house I watch Arend and Dad grilling fish at the barbecue, heads together, talking and nodding.

Miraculously everything arrives at the table simultanously: the fish, the chips and my yummy salad, served in small bowls so the littlies can't 'forget' to eat their greens. The talk is about Coral's debut as a cook. The chips are just right. 'You're a natural, me girl,' says Dad, winking at me. 'What is next on your menu?'

'One day I may try my hand at a special bread-and-butter pudding,' sighs Coral, rolling her eyes.

'Sprinkled with Australian gold dust. I just know I would make a great dessert chef one day. No greasy meat and sticky cookingpots for me! I'll be whipping up miracles with egg whites, crystallised fruit, choco-late and smoo-ooth mousses!' She smacks her lips, everyone laughs. Coral may be short but she is not a littlie any more. It's time we took notice of her talents and use them. Selfish brat that I am.

Just as I finish tidying the kitchen, after Yvan and Zora have washed and dried the dishes, I hear Dad speaking on the telephone. 'That you Bill? How's things? That's good! Say, is Patrick there? I'd like a word with him, thanks.'

I go cold at the mention of the name. Hell's bells, I hope Dad doesn't come straight out with what I told Arend!

'Hi there, Patrick. John Woodsman here. Long time no see. Yes … No … Not really. Say, Patrick, someone saw you riding up our driveway about mid-morning today. 'Cause you wouldn't have found anyone home at that time, seeing Tinka and Branka went to fellow-ship. But I wondered if you were looking for me? Anything I can help you with, Patrick … Oh, I see.'

Dad listens attentively. Clever Dad. He has kept my secret.

'Yeh, that is so, Patrick. We bought that strip of land, so I'm afraid you can't have it. Wouldn't be much use to you anyway, being so narrow. But added to our farm, well, that's different, isn't it. Well Patrick, sorry I can't oblige, but I hope you find some land for your purpose somewhere else. Have you tried the big island? … Yeh. Right you are. And oh, Patrick, remember, next time you want to see me 'bout something, just you wait with coming around till after sundown, when I'm home to receive you properly. Good day then.'

That's telling the rat! Dad sits down with a smirk of satisfaction on his face. So now we own the land that runs down to the beach and the cliff. Can't wait to go exploring!

'Guy wants to buy a beach of his own,' says Dad scathingly, 'as if he and his mob haven't done enough damage already! Good thing beaches are common property.'

'I reckon,' says Arend. 'That mob never put anything back into their land. People like him should have to do compulsory landcare courses before they're ever allowed to buy another acre.'

The Byderdike farm is an overgrazed, treeless property, misused. Our farm is paradise by comparison. But why are we so poor that we have to borrow from Auntie Branka to buy a strip of land, if Great-grandpa Arend owned a quarter of the island? We don't seem to have inherited any of it. All we have is Woodsman's land. I've heard it said that Grandpa Derek wasn't the best of managers and Grandma Barb a bit of a spendthrift. That's why we have a walnut wardrobe, two crystal vases, silk wall-hangings and lots of silver cutlery. But only two decrepit old cars.

I've never heard anything else but that the price of wool has hit rock bottom, or if it's up then so are the fees. Guess that's why we only have just enough land to raise crops and wool to buy what we need, and a lot of the time we eat what we produce ourselves. Like all islanders we live mostly on fish. Mum's family must have managed better, seeing Auntie Branka still has money in the bank.

The littlies play monopoly. 'I'm buying land,' shouts Yvan. For once he's not on the internet.

Dad laughs, lowering his paper. 'It's that sort of a day,' he says.

'If you can spare me I'd like to go to Sylvie Saturday morning,' I tell Mum.

'You mean to stay all day?' she asks. The usual wheeling and dealing.

'It's a long way to go,' I say. Sundew Cove is on the north coast. I have to cross the island from coast to coast. 'No use dropping in for half an hour and then have to turn back.'

Dad lowers his paper again. 'Bianka needs a day off to see her friend,' he says. 'She is too much cooped up in the house nowadays.'

'I should give Bianka driving lessons,' Arend puts in. 'If she rides Whoopsy to Sundew, I am grounded. Better if I could borrow the truck, Dad?' It's understood no one uses Mum's car, which is kept in good repair for emergencies.

'You can have the truck for the day if you bring Bianka to Sundew Cove and pick her up in the afternoon,' says Dad.

'That's two driving lessons, sis!' Arend is pleased. He wants to see his mates for a day. Mum doesn't put up any resistance when Dad weighs in. I guess she prefers him to take responsibility.

I ring Sylvie. The whole deal falls through if she has other plans. But she hasn't. 'Just hanging around the house this weekend,' she says. 'Hardly any homework 'cause I did it all last year. Let's go for yabbies.' Over the years Sylvie and I have talked the world together again while fishing for yabbies, though I never remember much of what we discuss. Yet I always feel better for it. I guess that goes for her too, having only two older brothers who stick together like bread and butter.

Auntie Branka rings her cowbell. I rush to her, because I should have brought cocoa half an hour ago.

'Sometimes it is quite frightening not to be able to move well,' says Auntie Branka. 'I was trying to be patient, because I know you have things to do, but I was getting withdrawal symptoms.'

'So sorry, Auntie!' I give her a hug. 'The kettle is on and I'll bring your cocoa in a jiff. Do you want anything with it? Or would you like to come to the lounge?'

'No, no, I have to finish my book. And I mustn't put on weight. You'd better halve the honey.' Dear old thing, she tries to maintain herself against the odds, but she loves her food and drink. I don't even know how old she is.

My thoughts turn to Tom Baudin. Is he better off, being mobile but living all alone with his memories that reach back into another time? When I carry in Auntie Branka's mug I sit down for a chat about this, that and nothing at all. When I walk out of her room ten minutes later, I'm sure she is light years happier than Tom Baudin.

'I'm going to read in my room,' I announce back in the livingroom and say goodnight to the family. It's nice sitting up in bed in my nightie, curtains drawn, wrapped in my quilt. But the library book lies unopened in my lap. So much to think about.

Today did not work out at all as planned, nor as the dawn had promised. All I meant to do was walk to Tom Baudin's cabin and find out who my great-grandmother was. I want to find a model for my own future life. Only last week I had ideas of grand independence day, but after today's events I wonder whether a girl can live alone at all. Should I take martial arts classes in Queenscape? But the whole island will know. All the guys will make jokes about it and a rat like Patrick Byderdike may want to test my prowess. I know and Dad knows that his talk about that strip of land was just an excuse. What if I do a course on Kangaroo Island? There must be one there if Platypus has it.

I make a mental note to buy *The Islander* when we collect *The Platypus Argus*. If I train Coral up a bit, I might be able to get away for a week to do an intensive course. Or do you need to go to the mainland for that?

This idea goes in the too hard basket just for tonight. What really bugs me is Flora. I had hoped to find a wonderful role model, so I could just follow in her footsteps and be guided by her spirit. But Tom's revelations have upset all that.

My mind rakes over the conversation, picking out what he said and what was left unsaid. Could it be that Flora fell in love at the drop of a hat, first with Arend, then with Tom? Did she prefer the comforts Arend offered to sacrificing it all for true love? And what of denying her son his true father? When the flak started to fall it landed on the poor kid's head as well. That must have been the main reason why he never returned to Platypus after boarding school.

Yet, she spilled the beans, Tom said, at a party some eighteen years later. Had she taken to drink? Not so easy to do when you live in isolated Sundew Cove. But I'd heard they also had a house in Queenscape at the time she left. Arend must have sold the homestead soon after. Queenscape has a well-stocked pub. Maybe she drank up Arend's fortune. If she did, it must have been a public secret. But so was her love affair with Tom. He said people hinted that Frederik was his son. They must have said like Ivy Rutt: 'And doesn't he have Tom Baudin's features? Same eyes. Same forehead.' Even though he looked like his mother. How could she possibly have stayed on Platypus?

I let that sink in. I try to be Flora. Try to imagine what it's like to have a big, strapping husband and know you have been unfaithful with a wild young man and are carrying his baby. What an incredible mess. But was it any worse than the three girls tripping up in Queenscape?

I try to imagine what Tom would have been like in those far-off days. Ruggedly handsome for sure, you see the traces even now. I still remember him with black curly hair. Tall and lean. And clever. Tom is a really clever man. Knows lots of things you never read about. Talks like a professor. You can see how attractive he must have been to beautiful, talented, creative Flora, who was probably bored to distraction by Arend and his pipe.

My thoughts drift from all the secrets uncovered today to the secrets created today. Even Dad was making up white lies on the phone to that wretch of a man, saying that someone had seen him go up our driveway. It seems you can't get by in life without twisting the truth here and there, because if you blurt out everything as it is, you could create more damage than anyone can fix up.

In my heart of hearts I know what I really think about Flora. She should have upped and left and gone to live with Tom Baudin, even if they'd had to leave the island. They could have been a happy family, like she was with her parents, and Arend could have married someone else. Oh! In that case Flora would not have been my relative at all! Nor would Grandma Barb have been the Barbara she was, having had a different mother. Dad would not have been the same dad, and we kids would have turned out differently. I could not have Flora Hammermeyer's straight nose and high cheekbones, or her talent for drawing. And if Arend had never remarried, someone else would have married Derek Woodsman and … Yipes! Extinct before we were born! Non-existence!

The family is getting ready for bed. Voices start up, floors creak, Dreadlocks whines for his dogbits, Auntie Branka's faint radio shuts down. I cannot imagine my family being other than they are. A chip of Flora is in all of us except Mum and Auntie, and I seem to have inherited quite a few of Flora's genes. Will I experience the same fatal attractions to lean handsome men as she did? Or will I be stronger? Times are different and women's lives are changing. But can a woman resist getting married as long as there are prowlers around? Am I trapped? Martial arts has to be the answer!

I stretch out to sleep, dead tired from a day like no other, having resolved nothing. House cleaning tomorrow. Independence day is further off than I imagined only a week ago. Role models. Do I need one?

6: The House at Sundew Cove

Arend and I bounce along in the truck on the Fiddlestick Cutting, the dirt road that crosses Platypus from south to north. When it was cut through the scrub they found stands of pink gum, manna gum and wattle and it is said the roadworkers made bows for their violins from the wood. There have always been fiddlers on Platypus, playing anything from old Irish or Celtic tunes to pop classics and fusion music.

'Where can I do an intensive course in martial arts, d'you know?' I suddenly ask Arend.

The wheel just jerks for a second. 'Intensive …? Yeh! I see what you mean. That Byderdike fella has really scared the daylights out of ya, has he?'

'I don't like feeling threatened,' I admit. 'But how can I get away for a week to do an intensive course? I have savings to pay the fees if it's not madly expensive.'

'But you don't learn martial arts in a week. It takes years! You'd have to go to the mainland. The bloke in Queenscape only teaches evenings and on Kanga it's just after school for kids.'

We drive on in silence. I feel depressed. Arend is trying to be helpful, but I feel so trapped. There seems no way I can do anything for myself!

'You thinking of leaving the island, sis?' asks Arend, his eyes on the road.

'I don't want to. It's just that I have to do something with my life and there seems no way that I can if I stay home forever.'

'Depends what sort of things you want to do.'

'If I could make choices without having to worry about my own safety from prowlers, things would be clearer in my mind,' I say, amazed how clear that actually sounds. 'Take today for instance. It was obvious Dad didn't want me galloping across the island on Whoopsy after he told off Patrick Byderdike about coming around during daytime. And to be truthful, I prefer riding with you in the truck, because if I met that creep here on the cutting, where could I hide? You can see people coming miles ahead.'

Arend glances at me sideways. 'I see your problem,' he says. 'I guess we blokes don't think enough about what it's like for women.' He is as thoughtful as Dad and maybe he can come up with a solution. 'I promise I'll give you regular driving lessons in the truck, come Monday. Being on wheels will help. You better take over now for a stint.'

'Thanks, brother! I don't know whether it's easier to be a girl on the mainland. All I know is that being an islander is cramping my style.'

'Forget about the mainland being easy living,' says Arend, stopping the engine and getting out. We walk around the car and I hoist myself into the driver's seat. 'You know how to start. There's the clutch, the brake, the accelerator. Take it slowly.'

I start the engine, push in the clutch and pull the gearstick into second, then carefully put my foot on the accelerator. There I go! Slowly. Just this straight bit of road. Concentrate.

'They're into drugs big time across the water,' says Arend, 'lots of unemployment, homeless kids, heaps of crime and crazies. It's not so bad here. Plenty of food, plenty of space. You have to work for it, but it feels good to be alive. I don't get that impression of mainlanders when I see the television news at my mate's place. Do you?'

'True,' I reply. 'I guess we have a great life here and I worry about a few restrictions. Yeh, well, just a few. But they stop me dead in my tracks just the same. I wonder who decided that everyone should have a regular job. What's wrong with living on a farm and feeding yourself?'

'Nothing as far as I can see!' says Arend with conviction, but then he falls into one of his sudden silences. He's thinking. He also gets that from Flora, I guess.

'There's the cove,' he says as we come over the saddle of a hill. 'Stop the truck!' I change back gears, switch off, pull on the handbrake. Standing on the road I look down on the cove.

The sight never fails to thrill me. One smooth, bald hill after another, still velvet green after the rain, hugging each other closely until they run into the brine of the sea. The homestead looks tiny from this height, lying snugly in a giant land fold from where Sundew Creek flows out to sea. Clumps of tall dark trees protect the house from gully winds.

I picture Flora in this vast landscape that dwarfs all human activity, painting trees, being a model wife and mother. A fairytale setting with the sea sparkling silvery blue in the V-shape between the two far hills. But she was no fairytale princess and the ending far from happy ever after.

Arend takes the wheel for the descent. Rumbling down the hill, I see Sylvie's dog Rover running through the front gate. And there are the remnants of Flora's native garden! As Rover barks Sylvie comes out, looking up, hands shielding her eyes against the sun.

'What time will you be back for me?' I ask Arend. He hangs on the wheel as we plunge down a forty-degree slope.

'Should be back by four-thirty, but don't worry if I'm a bit late,' he says. Arend is dependable. He will make some girl a terrific husband. Like Dad. You should be so lucky. I wave as he turns the truck, after an awkward greeting for Sylvie, and we watch him churn up the hill again.

'Let's grab some food and go,' says Sylvie. Walking up to the house is like approaching the entrance of a cave that seems to go deep into the earth between the hills looming like sleeping dinosaurs above us. The path is lined with limestone rocks and there are still big clam shells lying between succulent plantings and native groundcovers that Flora must have collected.

'I've been doing family history,' I tell Sylvie. 'Do you know who your family bought this property from?'

Sylvie holds open the flywire door for us to step in. 'From some foreign sailor guy. Long time ago, before Dad was born. Tell me more later.'

She pushes open the door to the great tiled kitchen and we raid the fridge for a picnic lunch. As she wraps up cheese, a cold sausage and crackers, I look around with new interest. Everything in this house is many degrees better than in ours. Ceilings higher, doors and passage wider, cupboards more numerous. Where there is wood it is bevelled or carved, not just planed. Where there are windows there is stained glass or small panes set in lead. Because of the size of the rooms the house has a slightly hollow ring. There is space for ghosts as well as the living.

'Ever noticed a presence in the house?' I ask.

'You mean ghosts?' Sylvie laughs her high clattering laugh. 'No, not me! But Christopher swears he saw a young boy wearing knickerbockers and a shirt and tie come into his room. That's years ago, but he still tells the tale.'

I freeze. Frederik. He's not even dead, but his childhood spirit has been haunting the house where he was born. 'Interesting,' I mumble.

Stuffing the pockets of our jackets with food and matches, we collect a bucket and scoop from the shed and follow the creek to the beach. Halfway is the waterhole where we collect yabbies. Talking is out, as the wind blows right at us. When we've scooped enough yabbies for a meal we make for the beach. The closer we get to the silvery V-shape, the stronger the wind. We hang into the gale like small yachts, jackets flapping, hair streaming, clutching our things. The salty air whistles in our ears, freezing the edges. Then, as we round a rock as large as a house, the wind falls away and the atmosphere is quite balmy. Through a tunnel of high rocks we reach the saltwater lagoon, our favourite spot for cooking the catch.

I realise today why talking to Sylvie makes me feel good. She is a good listener. I tell her my problems, minus the Flora and Tom saga, or the Byderdike incident. Just me and my future that is going nowhere.

'Yeah, well,' says Sylvie. 'I'm not so sure I know what I'm doing either. I thought university, but I am no more brilliant than last year. The new humanities teacher came up with a pretty good scheme though. You answer a list of questions with yes and no and then group the yesses and noes and it shows what sort of work you'll be happy doing for the rest of your life. Not what you're good at, but what makes you happy. She says that may well turn out to be the same, but it's a different way of looking at life, 'cause some kids can do anything, but not everything makes 'em happy.'

'What sort of questions?' I ask. 'And what did it say about you?'

'I'm suitable for anything to do with people, but

not in business or science or research. And I had planned to do biology, easier than the other sciences. The questions start by asking whether you want to work with lots of people, or a small team, or alone.'

'Alone,' I reply without considering the alternatives.

Sylvie turns to me. 'Gosh. That cuts out most jobs, Bianka! Teaching, nursing, shops, office work, army, police, Parks & Wildlife, you name it, you have to work with teams and crowds in all of them. You aren't becoming a hermit there on the farm, are you?'

'Farmers are lucky,' I grumble. 'They don't have to work with crowds.' I'm beginning to think I should simply stay where I am.

'Not lucky according to what my dad and my brothers keep saying every boring dinnertime,' snorts Sylvie. 'The wool price is always too low, there've been too many droughts and although beef does well, transport costs are rising.'

'Tell me about it,' I say. 'I hear the same stories. It really only means we aren't making a fortune like the early settlers, who got rich quick on everything they touched. But we survive, don't we? Nobody starves. How come, if things are that bad?'

'Don't ask me. I guess they have to complain about something. But I know for a fact that my dad told my mum to stop taking the ferry to the mainland to go shopping and quit looking through mail order lists. No holidays this year either. That means it's dead serious.'

'We hardly ever shop mainland or mail order and we haven't gone on holidays ever,' I reply. 'They say Platypus Island is as good a holiday destination as any in the whole southern hemisphere!'

We start acting out travel posters. 'The native girls of Platypus Island welcome you to romantic Sundew Beach,' Sylvie croons.

Stretching my hands under my chin, elbows in, I curve my back sideways. 'Learn the Platypus Island courting dance from real Platypus girls!' I purr and slide zig-zag along the water's edge. Then we demonstrate a wallaby hop. We roll laughing through the sand, thinking up more slogans to lure dark, handsome young men to the island for a stress break, until we get too silly for words.

'Maybe you could work in a call centre,' says Sylvie when we've stopped mucking about. 'Warehouses full of screens, every person working totally by themselves and you never talk to anyone except on the net.'

'I've hardly touched the home computer this year. I don't know that I want to sit at a screen all day. I'd go dotty.'

The sun has moved across the sky all too rapidly. Our raided lunch was munched along the way, but there's a good feed of yabbies in the bucket. I gather driftwood while Sylvie builds a fireplace between some rocks. We eat yabbies in silence before walking slowly back to the homestead, the wind in our sails.

'Write down those yes and no questions for me,' I

ask after we have shaken off the sand and cleaned up in the laundry.

In Sylvie's spacious bedroom we clear her desk. She gives me two sheets of paper and a pen and dictates: 'Put YES on one and NO on the other. Then write 'Alone' under YES and 'Crowd' under NO. The second question is 'Do you want to get rich or just make a living?'

'Just make a living,' I say and put it down under YES.

'I knew you'd say that,' says Sylvie. 'Most of the girls said the same and most of the boys want to get filthy rich. Mrs. Trapp said the girls were realistic and the boys overambitious.'

'True enough. What's next?'

'Do you prefer to work with your head or your hands?'

I waver. 'Both,' I decide.

'Then put 'head and hands' on the YES list.' Here, let me scribble out the rest and you can work it out at home. Then let's go look for mushrooms. There've been lots after the rain, so you can take a box home.'

I look over Sylvie's bookshelf while she copies the remaining questions, then stuffs the folded sheets in my pocket. As we leave through the back door carrying baskets, we pass the remnants of the free-standing stone studio.

'The roof has come off,' I say, looking up.

'Yeah. Gavin and Chris took it off to repair the top

of the walls and that is as far as they've gone. They ought to lay plastic on the floor tiles to keep them from getting damaged. Dad has given Mum one thousand dollars to redecorate the place for paying guests and he says not a penny more. But what can you do with a thousand dollars these days?'

I groan. Plenty, but I don't argue the point. Imagine what we could do with that sort of money to redecorate the verandah rooms for our paying guests!

We enter the studio through a doorless frame. The place has been used as a store room and looks pretty neglected. Sylvie leans on each window sill, looking in turn out to sea, at the hills and into a deep dark grove. Standing in the centre of the room, the walls begin to speak to me. My eyes are involuntarily drawn to a line of bricks under a window sill one metre from the floor. They stand out in the stone wall. As I look intently, the colour of one brick seems to darken, almost vibrate, inviting me too touch it.

'Let's go,' says Sylvie, picking up her basket and swinging through the door opening without looking back. I follow, passing the brick. I quickly finger it and it moves. One push and a tug and it gives. In a narrow cavity leans a small grey book. My breathing stops. Holding the brick with one hand, I lift the book with the other, slip it into the pocket of my jacket and push the brick back in. Then I run after Sylvie.

She hasn't noticed the delay. I feel hot and cold in turn and my neck and hands are sweating. I've stolen a book. But I am convinced it is Flora's possession and she hid it. Could it be her diary? I try to act normal as we come to where the mushrooms are sprouting.

For twenty minutes I listen intently to Sylvie as she tells her own tale of woe. She reckons she is so in love with a certain boy in her class that it interferes with her studies, but he has no eyes for her at all. That seems incredible. Sylvie is so pretty that she had to fight off boys all through high school. Maybe that's why she never gets very good marks. It isn't easy to be gorgeous. She's had half a dozen so-called steady boyfriends, none ever lasted, and now this desperate love for a nitwit of a guy with wax in his eyes.

Listening seems the best remedy, for Sylvie arrives at her own solution. 'You know, this heart throb could destroy my life if I let him, simply by doing nothing!' she says passionately. 'But I won't let any fella do that to me. So I'm going to take the initiative and invite him to dance with me at the next school dance. And if he won't then we don't and I'll give him up for good. It's time I start working for exams or I'll flunk!'

As we hug each other, Arend comes rumbling down the track. 'Ring me, Ringo!' sings Sylvie. 'Sure will, Sir Paul,' I shout back. Kidding like at school. But our problems are much, much more serious than last year.

'She got a boyfriend at the moment?' asks Arend when the truck climbs the hill.

'Hey, brother! You're interested?'

'Always thought her a nice girl,' Arend says tamely.

'Well, she hasn't. But it's the wrong time to ask her out now. I can't say any more.'

'Getya,' says Arend, his face lighting up a little. 'Keep me posted then, will ya?'

'For sure,' I promise. Who knows, Sylvie and Arend may be a good match. She bubbles, he simmers, but they're both honest and wouldn't it be wild if Sylvie and I'd become sisters!

But when I feel the hard cover of Flora's book against my chest I get frightened. Arend is great as a brother, but could he become dull and stodgy like the unhappy Arend Hammermeyer?

I get one more long stint at the wheel. Then we ride home in silence wrapped in our own thoughts.

7: Flora's Secret Diary

This evening I go to my room as early as I dare to be unsociable. But nobody misses me. My family seem to amuse themselves pretty well without me or a TV. Sylvie has television because on the north coast they get a good reception from the mainland. Down here it's still useless until the technology improves. We read books, play board games, talk, listen to our radios and walkmans or just laze about and think, while Yvan computes. Our hands sew, knit, whittle wood, make things from nothing much. Sometimes the whole family makes shadow animals on the wall with our hands. We do local fauna: platypus, wallaby, lizard, cockatoo and of course seals. Sometimes we hold debates about things we're all concerned about, like when we decided to take in paying visitors. A pretty primitive lifestyle, with rooms instead of caves and electric lights for torches. But I wouldn't have a lot of adjusting to do if I went to live in a cave on some uninhabited island.

I tidy my room, stack library books to be returned and hang away my clothes. Then I'm in bed with Flora's book in a paper wrap. This is the moment. But what if it has nothing to do with her?

I open the grey hardboard cover. A faded yellow violet is glued on the first page. Above it in that old-fashioned handwriting called copperplate it says 'Diary'. My hunch was right! Underneath the violet:

'Flora Patience Hammermeyer, 1947–'. No last date. Tom said she left about 1950.

The hard little book rests in my hands. What gives me the right to read her secret thoughts that she hid from prying eyes behind a loose brick in the wall! But then I recall the dream. Flora walking towards me with outstretched hands holding a small album. She offered it to me in the dream. But I was walking beside her. So was Frederik. What does it all mean? And hasn't she been dead since long before my birth?

I think for a while, Flora's diary in my lap, as if waiting for permission to turn the pages. I am no longer worried about having taken it. It would mean nothing to Sylvie's family and Flora would not want them to find it. She didn't know Arend would sell the place. I roll the dream past my mind's eye, like watching a movie for the umpteenth time. Always Flora's pose is the same: the flowing dress, hair in the breeze, eyes looking straight into mine, her outstretched hands offering the small album. To whom?

Then I hit on a strange and mysterious possibility. Could my intense desire to search her out have shaped my dream? Did I dream her up with the help of an old photograph? Could it be that I am leading Flora to myself so she can offer her secret thoughts? Would Frederik approve of my quest? But did he not transport his childhood self to Sundew homestead when he was lost in memories many years later, spooking Chris out of his room?

I do believe in the power of human thought. I read

half a book about it a year ago and it struck me as the most sensible thing I'd ever learnt from a book. Whatever happens, you can think your way through it and out of it. Now I feel strongly that I have permission to read Flora's diary – that she meant me to have it, long before I was born. Finding it behind the brick was a miracle meant to happen.

My fingers slowly turn the yellowing page when I notice the tip of a ribbon sticking out. I open the page where it lies. A pretty, faded mauve ribbon with pink and yellow embroidered flowers, used as a bookmark, lies where she stopped writing. The rest of the album is blank. I start once more at the beginning.

'Christmas 1947 – Warming up and the garden is at its best, but we'll give the presents in the drawing-room. Barbara expects tradition to be followed. She's ever so sweet, but adamant like her father, who insists on Scandinavian fare. I have given instructions to that effect to Cook. If I survive it all, I'll take the boat well before New Year to be with F. for January. Even sketching is a chore.'

'30th December 1947 – The sea was choppy, but the escape rivetting. The reunion with F. is worth any discomfort. His results are excellent. The master told me they want him to do advanced language and higher maths this coming year because he finishes class work before anyone else! I am so proud of him. He is a man beyond his tender years. If only T. would take an interest – it could have been arranged – but that is like wishing a rock would walk. He hasn't come off the island once. At any rate, I have long given up hope for support from that quarter. Tomorrow F. and I will do our yearly cultural excursion along the Terrace, where the buildings are cool. In a little street opposite the museum they serve a fine parfait with strawberries.'

So she went across leaving behind two men, neither of whom took an interest in her son. That's tough. Why couldn't Tom have visited his son on the mainland? He gives out to be such a proud father in his old age. I wonder who Cook was – did Flora have other servants? She led the life of a lady of leisure. A part of me hungers after such a life. What couldn't I do with leisure!

'2nd February 1948 – A. sent a telegram to fetch me home. Purportedly because B. is pining – that daddy's girl. So I am packing up and leaving my boy to start his new school year alone. We had such a grand time.'

She seems loath to go home. Didn't she love her daughter? I have a sudden flash of a long-lost memory. Grandma Barb washing Great-grandpa Arend's dead body. I can't have been more than five, maybe six, when I barged into that room without knocking. Her round little face was swollen and red from crying and she didn't survive him long. People kept saying she died so young, although she always seemed old to me. Before she died she grew so thin that Dad could lift her up in his arms to put her to bed, as if she was a child. She never seemed terribly happy, but she was very sweet to us kids and I bawled at her funeral.

A year later Grandpa Derek had a fatal accident

on Kangaroo Island, falling off a horse he wanted to buy. It bolted as a truck whizzed past. It was terrible. In a few years we lost the three eldest members of the family. Is that why Mum and Dad went back into production after Coral? If truth be told, Yvan looks exactly like Grandpa Derek, and Zora is a jollier version of Grandma Barb. Back amongst the living!

'15th March 1948 – A. has been so magnanimous. He has agreed to have my paintings printed as a book in a limited edition. I finished the one hundredth painting yesterday. Soon I must think of a new project to save my sanity.'

Tom said Frederik had the book published. Maybe that was a reprint, or did Great-grandpa Arend pull out? We don't even have one copy of that book in the family that I know of. She didn't write very often in this diary, only the highs and lows. Like this one:

'21st September 1948 – I think I shall go mad! The printer is forever delaying the proofs. A. tells me to be more patient, but he does not care about it the way I do! B. is indulging herself and growing puppy fat. It does not become her. I notified T. by posted letter of F.'s second term achievements – oh, the trouble I took to post it myself in Queenscape, quite unseen! Not a word of acknowledgement of course. The weather is dismal. My paint box has remained shut for weeks. I went for a walk to the cove in howling weather and longed for a cave on my dream island, where I might breathe unwatched and unfettered.'

Her dream island! Did she have a Sometime Island

fantasy of her own? A cave of her own? The simi-
larity with my own daydreams grips me by the throat,
almost stops my breath. How is it possible that two
lives, generations apart, can be so alike? It is almost
as if I am her ... or was her. As if she has become me.

I'm petrified! The thought rocks me. I have read
about reincarnation and who can tell whether bits of
people get recycled after they die? But what alarms
me is that the more I read her diary, the less I like
Flora. She seems rather cold and selfish, treating her
children quite unequally. And she doesn't seem to
love either Tom or Arend. Maybe it is unfair to judge
her by short entries in a diary, written at moments
when she was distressed and unhappy. I must read to
the end and hope to discover the real Flora.

'1st January 1949 – A new year and I have all my
resolutions handy, just as last year. I never keep them,
but it is traditional to mention them at parties for at
least two weeks. The only one I mean to keep is to
finish a hundred paintings of groundcovers in the four
seasons and persuade A. to pay for another volume.
The tree book is so handsome. People seem impressed
and surprised. I want but little from life these days but
to supply my paint box, don my cloak and brave all
but the wettest weather to roam the coast, the hills
and creek banks. If I discipline myself I shall become
quite famous with my books and sell the framed
originals through exhibitions. Already *Trees of Platypus
Island* is in the institute libraries on the mainland. I
receive letters from botanists and nurserymen. A. is

quite taken aback at the attention coming my way. As soon as I can get across, F. and I will travel on trains this holiday, with a stay in the Blue Mountains.'

No, she's not cold, because she must have cared about a lot of things to feel that now she wants but little from life. Maybe disillusioned is the word. She knows she's talented and seems determined to put all her energy into her work. But I don't like the way she schemes. Then again, if I were in her situation I'd probably badger old Arend daily to cough up for another book. Why not? Weren't they wealthy?

Here the thought of having a husband I do not love and who does not love me any more, falls around me like an invisible, smothering blanket. It's easy to blame Flora for the marriage going wrong, but I now understand she did not have the choice of taking her son and going to live with Tom, because Tom cut her dead! He fibbed when he hinted to me that she preferred comforts over him. I picture her sitting in her studio, year in year out, thinking of ways to reach the heart of the man she once had a secret romance with – sitting there at Sundew Cove, letting her thoughts turn sour while spinning rags of entanglements to snare Tom Baudin in his clifftop cabin to come down and rescue her. You'd think Tom would have been just that sort of knight on a horse, whisking away the love of his life to his rock and defying the world to point the finger. But he didn't, did he? He did nothing.

Have I ever heard of anyone doing a thing like that? Does it only happen in books and films then? I feel quite miserable from imagining the wasted years. Tom, Flora, Arend, Barbara and Frederik, all living loveless lives. Only Tom and Frederik are still alive. And as Tom never left the island as far as anyone knows, and no stranger has visited him on his rock or everyone would know, father and son never reunited. Maybe they write to each other, but nothing can make up for those long lost years.

I clap the diary shut to finish reading another time. Right now I don't want to know any more than I do already. Switching off the light, I turn on my left side for better dreaming and breathe deeply. But sleep will not come. Flora Hammermeyer keeps walking towards me with outstretched hands, offering her diary, while I skip beside her like her duplicate, her alter ego or whatever. I have become a split personality.

The words of Ivy Rutt return. How they shocked me. Until then I thought I was Bianka Woodsman, a unique human being, never seen before, with small but unique talents and my very own private dream of living in a cave on my secret island. Not even a week later I am reduced to just a carbon copy of my famous, witty, artistic, somewhat scheming great-grandmother, who incidentally disappeared mysteriously.

Several times I doze, waking up sweaty, my head stuffed with confusing images. Finally I must have slept. When I wake up with a sore head, the house sounds like Sunday morning.

8: The Jobs Test

Sunday is much like other days, just later and lazier. I supervise the littlies eating breakfast, clean up, help prepare food for the rest of the day and share a coffee with whoever is still at home by ten. Usually that's Mum and Dad, Auntie Branka and Zora. Today, Yvan, Coral and Arend leave to watch a basketball match at Manna Creek. I used to be in a team, but they have written me off. I don't miss it – it was just something you did at school. I prefer going walkabout.

Sunday is the day I reinvent myself. I look back at the week, what went wrong, what went right. I seldom make tremendous discoveries, nor get big surprises – I just count the little gains. But this week has caused some stupendous turnabouts. Nothing went to plan, I made some incredible discoveries and had one nasty experience I could have done without. This was the week I was going to prepare for independence day, talk to Mum and Dad. Big laugh. After what I've been through this week, last week's ideas seem kid's stuff. Now I'm much less sure of myself.

I carry the coffee tray to the big window, where we all snuggle in deep chairs, looking out on the orchard in bud. Love the smell of freshly brewed coffee.

'We'll have to invest in netting this spring,' says Dad, sipping. 'Or the birds will get the better of the fruit. I don't want those popguns about, they are noise pollution.'

'You'd better do it then,' says Mum, 'and don't delay.' Mum has excelled herself. While I was away yesterday she took back her kitchen and baked these crunchy peanut biscuits and a sponge cake. Mum is a terrific baker whereas I am ignorant beyond plain bikkies and a quiche.

'Am I imagining it, or do you look tired?' Dad asks as he peers at me. Sharp-eyed man.

'Didn't sleep too well,' I reply. He probably thinks I am having PMT and leaves it at that. But no.

'Mum and I have been thinking about your situation, lovie. Mum's worried you work too hard and don't go out to see your friends. You used to have so many friends when you were at school. Have they all left Platypus?'

'Yep, most of 'em. But they weren't all best friends, Dad. I'd miss Sylvie if she left, but now she thinks she won't make it to university next year.'

'It's that tough, eh?'

Mum butts in. 'Bianka, I feel a lot fitter than I did last year and if there's any course you want to do next year, let's talk about it. Coral can be quite a good help at home, she's fifteen.'

'Yes, let's do a little planning,' adds Dad. 'Coral is no great academic and I'm not going to keep her at school against her will after Year Eleven. That would be a waste of everyone's energy, teachers included. But you have always had ideas of further study, haven't you?'

Again I'm taken by surprise. When will it stop? 'I

haven't made up my mind yet, Dad. I'm getting close, but give me a few more weeks. I'm learning to drive right now and it's only September. Sylvie gave me a list that her teacher uses to test people's abilities. I am going to test myself today.'

'Good,' says Dad.

'Don't leave it too long then,' says Mum.

'And if you want to do something unusual, my child, you must put it on the table,' says Auntie Branka. I know that means she'll finance anything within reason.

'I might want to become a professional ...' I want to crack a joke, but can't think of anything. 'Oh, I don't know! If I could knit like you I'd become a professional knitter, Auntie!'

She holds up the nearly finished cardigan for Mum. She's doing the neckband and it looks very stylish. 'Will you use wooden buttons, Auntie?'

'Yes, yes. Arend collected some good sticks to slice up.'

Mum looks pleased to be wearing it soon. We sip the rest of our coffee and then I announce I'm going for a walk till lunchtime.

'If you see any everlastings, Bianka,' Auntie Branka sings out as I stand by the door, 'bring me just a little posie with some gum leaves, round ones.'

'Will do. Any orders for wattle? It's still out everywhere.'

'Don't!' cries Mum. 'It spills pollen.'

Outside I push my hands deep in my pockets and march off. Going to reinvent Bianka Woodsman. Rescue what is my own from a collision with an intrusive ancient relative!

Two grey wallabies hop across my path; a flock of galahs fly out of the scrub, first grey, then rose-pink as they turn on the wing. In the distance the moaning navigation cries of corellas. A crow makes a lot of noise in the sky and throwing back my head I see it attacking a wedgetail eagle twenty times its size. Brave little policeman of the air!

Walking here it seems nothing ever changes. Smelling the sea and boronia shrubs, listening to the cries and trills of wild creatures, feeling my blood pump nicely and rhythmically as it ought to. Straight ahead is the new strip of land Dad bought. Hey! I can cross it and be at the beach in no time.

I start to run, reinvention forgotten. Haven't been to that beach for ages because of having to walk around the long way and Dad warning us not to make trouble with the owner by trespassing. Whoever he was. I duck our fence and sprint across the new land until I start panting. I feel alive! The gentle rise levels out to a flat place before the land plunges and there is the ocean. Running down the dune I come to a stop on the wet sand amid debris washed up by the tide. The waves recede wearing lacy foam caps. Far away, between streaks of turquoise and blue waters, I imagine Sometime Island. Wish it were real. But if it was, some real estate developer would already have bought it for a remote resort.

I inhale deeply. And again! This is living! Smells of sea, sand, kelp and fishes. Prickly grains of sand thrown in my face by the wind. On solid wet sand I start running towards the cliffs. At the foot of the first cliff I sit down on a dry rock and watch the water trying to wet my shoes. Little crabs drift past, waving arms to find an anchor. Gulls skim across the low water looking for them. Run little crab, run! You're too young to be eaten whole. Eat and be eaten, that's life at the shoreline. Everywhere else, too, I begin to realise. Running my fingers through water and sand, I imagine living here as a hermit. I'd love to go for a swim, plunge into the waves. But the water is still freezing.

Further on a jumble of jagged rocks is exposed during low tide. I led Stephen across to the first cave last year. You can see it from here. It's as far as I've ever climbed, because I always sit in the cave so long that the tide turns and I have to clamber back to the beach in a hurry. When I get a whole day to myself I shall venture further.

Slowly I walk back, looking out to sea in case Sometime Island pops up. Nothing else between here and Antarctica. Years ago we heard on the radio that a woman doctor in Antarctica discovered she had breast cancer. When Mum came down with the disease I remembered the woman in Antarctica, waiting for the plane to drop medicines. In early spring they picked her up. We may be isolated, but not like that. Mum must be doing alright if she claims she can let me go next year. She must have noticed my restlessness. But now I realise it's not so much a desire to leave, but to know. Know who I am, what I am going to do and be.

I turn back to land. This afternoon I'll test myself with Sylvie's questions. No decisions. Just do the test and see what it adds up to. Live with the outcome for a few days. I nearly step on two white everlastings, but I won't pick any unless I see a colony – to save the species. It's the wrong path for gums, so I pick some grevillea for background. Before I reach home I find plenty of everlastings.

'You darling!' cries Auntie Branka, waxing lyrically over the tiny red grevillea flowers and the music straw-flowers make when she runs her fingers across the petals. I wheel her to the big table before I set it for a lunch of bread with fried mushrooms. She puts the little vase of flowers in the middle. One by one the littlies tumble in, then Arend.

'Sylvie gave me this for you,' he says. 'She thinks you dropped it yesterday.' In his hand lies a piece of ribbon, identical to that in Flora's diary.

I feel the blood rise to my cheeks and wonder who notices. 'Oh thanks,' I mumble, taking the ribbon and stuffing it in my pocket. Is Flora Hammermeyer going to send me daily reminders of her existence? I slam a knob of butter in the fry pan to make it sizzle and slice the mushrooms. There must have been two ribbons in the diary.

Mum puts a bowl of apples and oranges on the table, milk for the kids, lemon cordial for us. She cuts slices of rye and wholemeal bread, putting one of each on the littlies' plates. By the time I come to the table with the first batch of fried mushrooms, it matters no longer whether I look hot and bothered. Only later do I realise that Arend talked with Sylvie at basketball. Oh shucks! But it's not my business if he wants to get his emotions messed up. I warned him not to.

As soon as I can excuse myself I escape to my room. Spreading out two sheets of paper, I rewrite the headings YES and NO. The list of questions reads:

1. Do you prefer to work with a crowd of people, a handful, or alone?

2. Do you want to become rich, or make a reasonable living?

3. Do you prefer to work with your hands or your head?

4. Do you prefer to go out to work, or work from home?

5. Are you prepared to keep studying for your chosen work, or not?

6. Are you monolingual, bilingual, or multilingual?

7. Do you like frequent travel or staying in one area?

8. Are you or will you become computer-literate?
9. Would you prefer to work with people, animals or plants?
10. Do you prefer working indoors or outdoors?
11. Do you prefer to be involved with technological or scientific projects?
12. Would you like to become your own boss, or rather work for one?

I think hard about the questions. Some I have never considered. I'd always vaguely thought I'd like to travel one day. But frequent travel for work? I don't think I'm cut out for that at all. So I end up with two lists:

YES	NO
Work alone.	Not with a crowd or a handful.
Make a good living.	No need to become rich.
Work with my hands.	Prefer not to go out to work.
Work with my head.	Neither bi- nor multilingual.
Prefer to work from home.	No frequent travel.
Prefer to keep studying for my work.	Not very computer-literate.
Monolingual.	No technological talent.

Prefer working in one area.
Want to become more computer-literate.
Prefer working with plants or animals.
Prefer working outdoors.
I like scientific projects.
I'd love to become my own boss!

When I read through the NO list I regret I never took a language. I couldn't see the point of learning Japanese or German then or now. Yet, I would have loved to put down 'bilingual'. I definitely must get more computer skills, because it is fun and it's bound to be really useful for a host of jobs.

Reading the YES list I feel very strongly about my answers. A picture of me emerges. The only surprises are that I'd prefer to work from home rather than going away, that I'd prefer working with plants when they put the question the way they did, and as an afterthought with animals. That means outdoors I guess, but perhaps not really with Parks & Wildlife. And that I'd love to be my own boss! Well, fat chance. You need capital for that, or lots of luck. Still, having worked through the test makes me feel positive. I'm getting a handle on what I'd like to become. I'll keep rolling the YES list around in my head until it starts to gel. Maybe a job idea will just roll out, like a computer print-out.

I'll sleep on it. Tomorrow we go for supplies, change library books and choose vegetable seeds for my spring garden.

Mum and I come home loaded with news and some real gossip after our trek to the general store and the library agency. The island is buzzing with a delicate little scandal. Meek Mr Taylor left his wife last month and went off with sweet Mrs Spinner. It is said they eloped to New South Wales. Bossy Mr Spinner visited naggy Mrs Taylor and told her to call her husband to order. But as they talked things over, they found they agreed about so many things that they sort of fell in love! Or at least they decided to cut their losses and start something new together!

If that wasn't incredible enough, over the weekend Mrs Spinner and Mr Taylor returned to Platypus. It is said Mrs Spinner was left sitting on a seaside bench at Queenscape, while Mr Taylor went to tell his spouse he'd made a mistake and was coming home! Of course Mrs Taylor wasn't home. When after enquiries he found her in Mr Spinner's well-appointed two-storey house, Mrs Taylor and Mr Spinner said: 'Too late, mate!' Mrs Taylor stayed in Mr Spinner's house. So Mrs Spinner had to move in with Mr Taylor for somewhere to stay, but it is rumoured she wants her share of the Spinner furniture or the money, so she can live on her own or take a passage across to start a new life. It's funny how many people come to the islands to start a new life, but if islanders need to start again they do it on the mainland.

People – they make you blink! Love doesn't seem

to last a lifetime for a lot of people. I remembered Flora of course and her second love for Tom which did not stand the test of time either. Finished loving at twenty-one and never tried or dared to try again. Think not twice but a hundred times before you leap. But how can you know? People in love are always so certain!

Mum was suitably scandalised by the drama and said people talked too much. But how could anyone possibly ignore this? How could you say matter-of-factly: 'Hello Bevan and Mavis, good to see you!' if at an earlier meeting you'd said to the Spinners: 'Hello Bevan and Daisy, how are you keeping?' Wouldn't that be daft!

I wonder what people said about Flora Hammermeyer at the time. Will I ever find out? She won't have recorded that in her diary!

I said I felt sorry for Daisy Spinner, who seems to be the big loser. 'Please stop talking about it,' Mum grumbled. There wasn't much more to be said anyway.

9: A Week of Chaos

I bought ten packets of vegetable seeds, including combo lettuce and Japanese greens – wish I could read the packet. Tomorrow I start digging beds. Not a bad batch of books. I had ordered a new one on plants of Platypus Island and it was in today's parcel.

I wonder whether modern writers consult Flora's books? Quickly I look up the bibliography, running my finger down the authors' names. There she is! 'Flora P. Hammermeyer: *Trees of Platypus Island, South Australia*. I go strangely hot and cold at this real evidence of my great-grandmother's existence out there in the wider world. I browse while Mum drives, eager for more telltale signs of Flora's work.

We collect the mail at the gate. At home we have coffee with Auntie Branka, sharing around books and seeds. Mum sorts the mail. A pile of bills for Dad and a letter for herself. She opens and reads it.

'The Crackmans want to come for ten days this month instead of the long vacation,' she says with a note of alarm in her voice. 'Stephen is shifting to Canberra university and he needs the summer holiday to find a flat and settle in.'

I feel the bottom drop out of my being. I haven't thought about Stephen for a week, being so pre-occupied with Flora and my own life. But it always sits in the back of my mind that he'll come for a whole month in summer and we'll walk and talk and catch up with each other's world. Okay, he's still coming, but the Canberra shift tells me that his world and mine are parting company like two parts of a splitting iceberg. Why would an independent uni student want to share ideas with the house drudge who washes his towels and serves his meals? Because that's what I will be doing when they come. I never minded doing it while we were both school students, but now it'll be different and I do mind. I'm becoming a reverse snob!

'We'll have to start shifting things around come Friday,' says Mum. 'And I haven't finished that double quilt for the guest room.'

'Why worry about that,' I say brusquely. 'They don't know you're making it, so they won't miss it. And now, if you'll tell me what you want for tea, I'll do the vegies and then take an hour off to read my new book.'

Mum is visibly upset by my tone of voice. 'I don't want you to feel your time isn't your own any more, Bianka,' she says stiffly. 'You can go and read now. Branka and I can prepare the food.'

Leaving without a word, books under my arm, I flop on my bed, door shut. I do feel that my time isn't my own any more – Mum ought to realise that from the amount of work I do. And now the full impact of Stephen's changed life hits me.

Last summer rushes back, down to that last attempt

to kiss. They had come straight after Christmas, so Stephen and I had five weeks to renew our acquaintance and deepen our attachment. Was it love?

A really devastating thought strikes me. Until now I'd secretly thought Stephen and I were a little in love. But if I were truly in love I wouldn't be able to think past the moment of his arrival, when we see each other again after nearly eight months. Nothing would matter except that I would hear his voice close to my ear.

Instead, I am being so realistic about our relationship that I'm already depressed even before he arrives! Don't I care enough for him to be happy about whatever is good for his future? I've never thought it through. Am I envious? Maybe I too want to be an independent student at a university, studying botany and agricultural science, dancing at a student bash, taking part in debates on topics of national interest and the environment.

Is that really me? Not according to the YES list, except for studying. Am I simply jealous because Stephen's life is going to be lots of fun, apart from the hard yakka? While I drown in drudgery? I'm a jealous bitch. And I bitched at Mum, who is trying to give me up so I can have a life of my own. It's up to me then, isn't it? Nobody is trying to stop me, for goodness sake!

Done the whole circle. Back at me and my hurt feelings. No solution in sight. I feel mad, mad, mad.

And cheated, though I don't know by who or what. Might as well read and calm myself down. I open the first book of three.

Plants of Platypus Island, written by someone whose name I've never heard. Not an islander. Auntie Branka would have a thing or two to say about that. 'There's two kind of visitors,' she always says. 'The kind that pays and the other kind that gets paid.' Those that get paid are the researchers, the penguin counters and the yakka specialists, the soil and weather testers, the archeologists and shipwreck divers. Then there's the postcard photographers and the book writers, who come and go, never to be seen again.

Dad would laugh and say: 'Branka, these people are doing something good for Platypus. Make us famous. Bring more visitors of the paying kind.'

But Auntie would growl: 'I cannot see why local people can't count penguins, measure yakkas, take the best pictures and write books about Platypus. We known more about it than anyone else.'

'Go ahead and write a book then, Branka,' Dad chided her and Arend added: 'Maybe we locals cannot see the trees for the forest. Visitors notice things we simply drive past. We take Platypus for granted and take too little interest in our environment.'

He's only partly right because some of us do take an interest, himself included. This is a pretty good book. You could never take such flower pictures with our little camera. What sort of camera would you need? Most of these plants I known by sight, but I had no idea that bees shun the brown-throated cygnet lily, really an orchid and only found on Platypus and Kanga. The wildflowers will be at their best early October. I'd love to own a book like this. Could ask one for my birthday. Dad might phone up the Adelaide bookshop and have the courier pick it up. Or I could write now and have the information ready at the right moment. I have the shop's address somewhere. Perhaps I could become a native garden designer like Flora … do a course. But who would pay to have their plot laid out by me?

I find paper and envelope and write to *The Book Lover*, at the postbox address in Adelaide, asking for the price of this title, quoting author and publisher. When I'm done I have conquered my mood of despair. The littlies are coming up the driveway. Dreadlocks is barking for joy. I should go in and give a hand with things.

A galeforce wind that was forecast has just picked up. The door slams when the kids come in. 'Bianka, the wind is blowing down your peas!' shouts Zora.

Blast! I run outside to the rescue and nearly get hit on the head by a flying piece of masonite. Why can't the men batten things down?! Fury rises again inside me. In the patch there is nothing left to rescue. The flimsy wooden rack I hammered together myself has blown over and my beautiful tall snowpeas lie mangled and broken in a sorry tangle. I'll never sort them out without breaking the stems. Best to pick all the pods when this storm is over and start again.

Dad and Arend drive up in the truck and I shout about the masonite. Arend runs to put a brick on it and does a quick check for other loose items. We all make it to the door just as big drops start pelting down. Dad rubs his hands. 'Just what the doctor ordered,' he says.

'It could have waited till I'd dug my beds,' I complain. But rain is always welcome and I'll just have to wait till things dry out a bit. That won't be for a few days from the sound of that volume the sky is letting loose.

After the meal and cleaning up, I keep myself focused by drawing a master plan for the spring and summer vegetable garden. I want to do something completely different. Tripods for climbing beans. Dig them in a foot deep, a row of them. Get Arend to help me. He does almost anything for me if I pretend not to know how to go about it. I'm as calculating as Flora when it suits me.

Then I want to make a round central bed for brown and green lettuce, radish, rocket, mustard and spring onions. A one-stop salad shop. The Japanese greens grow tall, so they can go where the broad-beans are. The beans are also ready to be picked after this battering. Auntie will pod and pack them for the freezer. Cabbage here, broccoli and caulies there. And I'll grow herbs between the vegetables instead of separately. The strong aromas may put off a few munching critters. Must transplant those herbs before it gets hot.

Another part of my mind is watching how I prevent myself sliding back into depression. There are so many things I like doing, so why not do them? I adore planning. I would make a great garden designer, if only there were people on Platypus who could afford to hire me. Maybe there are a handful.

By the time I go to bed I'm fine. Just fine. Even looking forward to seeing Stephen Crackman next week. Of course. Why not. Enjoy the good things that come your way. Take life as it comes.

The days of the week fly by with doing damage control after the storm and preparations for the Crackmans' arrival.

Dad repairs and puts back the dividing door in the corridor that makes the two best rooms of the house a separate flat. Any junk dropped in the covered verandah is returned to its sloppy owners, mainly Coral and Yvan. Their toys and clothes are packed in boxes and shifted to Mum and Dad's room. Arend and I make space in our rooms to accommodate camp beds, cramping our style.

During summer we live so much outdoors that nobody minds, although Yvan and Coral must have their computer corner for homework. This time we do all this shifting for just ten days. But money is money, says Mum. She hopes the Crackmans will return next year, with or without their son.

Throughout the carting, cleaning and digging I am as restless as a cuckoo trying to drop her egg in another bird's nest. I want to offload all this domesticity, this eternal round of housework. Gardening and cooking is okay and at least you get to eat it. But I am sick of housekeeping, and cleaning is the pits even with the radio on full blast. I guess there's just too many of us living in a small house, soon even smaller for ten days of Crackmans. Will we get a booking for the long vacation in their place? If not, we shall be short of cash next year.

In the middle of the chaos Dad and Arend take off for Queenscape one day, in a cloud of mystery. When they return they won't say what they've been up to, but look mighty pleased with themselves.

'Hang on a week or so and all will be revealed,' says Dad when I ask whether he had an interesting day. The next day they come home bespattered with mud, looking even more smug and just as evasive. We must be a secretive family by nature.

10: Messages from the Past

The next day two truckies break down near our gate and come up to borrow a tool. Dad says lunch is just being served and they're welcome to join in. Lunch is usually bread and soup and that happens to be borscht, Auntie Branka's favourite Russian beetroot soup.

The blokes blink in disbelief, but they are very polite and carefully dip their spoons in to take a small sip of red broth. Auntie chuckles when they say in surprise: 'Hey, this ain't half bad,' and 'Well, I'll be beetroot!' They tuck into buttered ryebread with sheep cheese and have a second helping of borscht. In between they tell us Mrs Spinner is in an almighty stew and Mr Spinner can't go to the pub for fear of being accosted by the locals.

We hear more of the saga of Spinner and Taylor when two neighbours drop by to swap fresh meat for honey. Turns out it isn't true that Mrs Spinner moved in with Mr Taylor for somewhere to stay. That was just a rumour that grew as the idea of the possibility passed from mouth to mouth. In truth, Mrs Spinner remained sitting stubbornly on a wooden bench under the trees that line the shore in Queenscape, looking out to sea, clutching her handbag, carrybag at her feet. When neighbours got wind of what was happening – news really flies on the wind here on

Platypus – they rushed to her aid. But she wouldn't go with them as they lived next door to Mr Spinner and her ex-lover's ex.

In desperation one neighbour fetched policeman Ray Darcy to reason with Mrs Spinner. People had started to gather, because everybody knows everybody and somebody who could know said that what Daisy Spinner had endured from her husband would make a stone weep. Then someone suggested to go around with a hat and put Mrs Spinner up in the Sea & Salt for the night until things cooled down.

That is what happened and the same evening a support group was formed to help Mrs Spinner start a new life if she so wished. A few archenemies of Bevan Spinner were in it. They said the fella had always bullied his wife around and they were not at all surprised that she refused to return to the matrimonial torture chamber to ask for help.

Other supporters expressed the opinion that Mrs Spinner should forget about asking for a share of the furniture, but get a lawyer and claim half of the entire estate, contents and all, as blood money for twenty-four years of silent suffering. It's rumoured that Daisy Spinner's life became totally unbearable since the Spinner daughter left home at a tender age.

Evidently a generous sum was collected to maintain Daisy for a while and although the hotel manager did not want to admit this, it is thought he is donating the room for the duration of the off-season. Which isn't long, but it shows what islanders will do when one of them is in deep trouble.

Later in the week Dad heard along the road that Mrs Taylor had left Mr Spinner, saying it was all a big mistake, and returned to Mr Taylor. Men catch more gossip than women on Platypus, since they drive around a lot and stop when meeting friends. You often see two parked trucks, nosing opposite directions, drivers yarning until the cows come home or other traffic hoots them on.

So this year's big drama on Platypus is fizzling out and things are just about back to normal. Only Daisy Spinner will be spinning off into orbit very soon. I'm not being callous. I do feel dreadfully sorry for her. Mum keeps saying 'How's the poor dear going to manage on her own on the mainland? He never even let her go visiting alone.' And I say: 'How can any woman let herself be so bullied for so long? That's what I'd like to know.'

Apart from gossiping about the Spinner affair, our men come home another day with the news that some mainland developers are keen as mustard to cut up a farm they've just bought into a hundred little plots with cabins, a family resort. It's going to have a mini-golfcourse, tennis court, soccer field, club house and even though it lies within cooee of the sea, a swimming pool.

Quality up-market development they call it. Dad says it's good agricultural land and water going down the drain, in exchange for more pollution. A group of locals are mounting a campaign to stop council approving the plan. 'We will win,' Dad says. 'We've won before. And we may buy it off those guys as communal land to farm in rotation, to keep it in the Platypus family so to speak.'

I guess the council members know very well it's the rate payers who elect them who do the hard yakka. The islanders, almost to a man and a woman, don't want tourist development like on the mainland.

'We want Platypus to be an island with real island hospitality,' proclaims Dad and starts dialling a batch of neighbours to stir them up. 'Flipping city developers got their claws on Joe Stagesie's property,' he shouts into the phone, 'and they're going to ruin the bed and breakfast country-style hospitality of Platypus if council lets this through!'

'Ah!' says Auntie Branka, 'so now we're having activists on Platypus! Right here in the family!'

'You bet!' says Dad and Arend puts in: 'Haven't we always been? Aren't we the ones that do the work? We can't afford to laze around in a resort. We only cater for those who can.'

Discussing the development around the table, we get so enthusiastic about our own brand of island hospitality that we pledge to give the Crackmans the best our humble farm has to offer. They are coming into the horn of plenty. The ducks have just begun to lay, I have a supply of geese eggs in the fridge for baking, there's plenty of honey, enough matured sheep cheese if we ration ourselves, winter vegetables galore and fish whenever they crave it. Coral suggests salad platters with cheese or fish and radishes cut into stars. Mum and Auntie plan to bake supplies of cakes, biscuits, scones, fruit pies and apple strudel. Good for us. There is always plenty left over!

But one event really lights up this chaotic week for me. Months ago Dad brought home lottery tickets for all of us, in aid of the Queenscape Memorial Hospital. I can't quite believe it when Mrs. Ivy Rutt rings up on behalf of the hospital auxiliary and asks to speak to me.

'Bianka Woodsman,' she rasps in her aggravating voice, 'you are the lucky winner of the second prize. A return trip to the mainland on the Sea Horse ferry, to be taken up within the next six months. You lucky girl!'

I thank her twice in exactly the same words: 'That's really great, Mrs. Rutt, thanks a million!' I just can't think of other words. Never won anything. Can't remember ever holding a lottery ticket either. Having bundled up my room for the littlies to move in, I don't even know where the ticket is. I spend half an hour going through cartons until I find it where it ought to be, in my wooden treasure box with friendship bracelets, lucky stone, foreign coins and my first baby tooth set in silver.

'When are you going to leave us?' Dad asks jokingly at dinner.

'I've got six months,' I reply, 'and I can use it only once. So I'll think of a really good reason to go across.'

'That's my girl,' says Dad and I notice Mum looks distinctly relieved. So she isn't all that sick of me after all.

'I've never won anything,' complains Coral.

'Can I carry your bag?' jokes Yvan.

'I like mainland shops,' sighs Zora, dreaming of silk gowns and high-heeled beaded shoes.

And Arend says: 'Better start earning your spending money, sis, 'cause they aren't giving you that, are they?'

Then Dad's voice, sharply: 'Bianka has already earned her spending money well and truly. It will be ready for her when she is.'

Everybody looks at me with a new sort of respect. I feel my cheeks flushing for being the centre of attention. It seems I'm more appreciated than I realised. 'Thanks, Dad,' I mumble.

What to use the precious return fare for? I haven't a clue. Where can I stay on the mainland? Being islanders from way back, we don't have relatives there. Yet, it's pretty exciting to have won something valuable. Lady Luck is smiling at me in this period of stagnation in my island life.

With only two nights of privacy left, I read the rest of Flora's diary in bed. Sometimes she refers to events and people that raise an echo because they are the usual island events and characters. She mentions births, deaths and marriages, but almost nothing about herself during 1948, as if she has no life of her own any more. Then in 1949, although the entries are as short and sporadic as before, she writes about no one else but herself, in a new and strange way.

'I sat in utter bliss at the cove today. Don't know how long I was there. The sun must have moved from my right to my left, but as it also shone from inside me, I did not realise the passing of time until it grew dark. Then I woke up to the cold.'

Very mystical. There are similar passages of her walking, painting, sitting, even singing, always in a sort of timeless way. In September she writes: 'My pain has dispersed to merge with the agony of all living beings. Life serves up so much suffering that we must drink its beauty to the full.'

Not until December does she mention her children: 'I have stitched my motherly love into a pretty nightgown for B. for Christmas. A. has at last decided she can go to boarding school. She will be near F. who will keep a brotherly eye on her – just two streets away. A. seems to be sinking into permanent contemplation of … what? Yet I am closer to understanding him now than ever before.'

In the first three months of 1950 there are more short entries about bliss, peace of mind and something she calls 'the integration of body, mind and cosmos.' This is high-faluting stuff – I like it. I do not feel a stranger to her words, even though she doesn't reveal what is happening in her life that makes her feel this way. Unless it is the experience of what she calls 'the keen ache of loving everything' in 1948, when she decided to love trees and rocks, the sun and moon, flowers and insects and everything else on an equal footing, because just loving people never brought her happiness. 'I even begin seeing A. as a deciduous tree, who gave shelter for a few seasons. That makes it easier to respect his withdrawal into dormancy.'

What a stunning thought! I play for a while turning people into trees. Tom is a knotty old coastal pine and Gary of the Bay Shop a flowering gum because he blossoms in cold weather. But there is no tree I would insult so much as to compare it to Patrick Byderdike! I don't have Flora's tolerance.

Then, in April: 'Goodbye trusted diary.' Yet going on several pages she writes: 'The Sisters replied from Tas. There will be a humble place for me when I have seen to F. and B.'s holiday arrangements. A. lives in a world of his own. I should never have married. It has nothing to do with him, I can see that now. But how could I have known myself at seventeen? Or indeed at twenty, when T. walked in and out of my life. The one who loves me no longer does not want to let me go, the other who claims to love me does not want me in his life. I cannot make either happy. My love for them, brief and insubstantial as it was, has finally grown into an undemanding love for all that lives, loves and suffers. Without these two men this might not have happened. Had I married happily in Tasmania, I might now be slightly bored, but too grateful for my security to change a thing. Instead, I am leaping into the unknown. The cloister is not an escape, but the greatest adventure I have ever dared contemplate. My remaining paintings and possessions will be sent to auction, my clothes given away and there will be nothing left of young Flora who searched for happiness but the imprint of my foot on the sands of Sundew Cove. One high tide will wash that away as well. Then the world will have one more nameless worker to help relieve human suffering. Tomorrow's P.I.C.K. social in Queenscape will be the stage of my farewell.'

So they had P.I.C.K. even then! The light keepers, living on their cliffs and capes became the Platypus Island Coast Keepers, looking out for smugglers, ships in distress and storm damage. They still do, but now they mostly report illegal fishing vessels, oil slicks and other environmental damage. Everyone living on the coast is automatically a member and we still have the social once a year for all the families, about half the island. What is Flora up to at the P.I.C.K. social?

'Both A. and T. will be there. I am gathering my courage to say in public what I have memorised, to give each their own reason to want to see me go forever from their lives. Goodbye Platypus. I never reached that other island I dreamed of so often, but return to the home island instead.

'P.S. – I leave this diary to be found by whom it may concern. My children must not see it. May it be found by one who can use a message from a miscalculated life, in ways I myself cannot yet fathom. Perhaps it will be unearthed by a descendant of my dear and only daughter, for whereas I was not the marrying kind and did, she is the marrying kind and will. Of that I am certain, but of not much else.'

As if struck by lightning I sit bold upright in bed in the sleeping house, Flora's diary on the quilt. All week I've been scheming how to put it back behind the brick in the studio at Sundew homestead, because I still felt I should not keep it forever. And here she points the finger at me, descendant of Grandma Barb, who was the marrying kind and lived her life for Grandpa Derek, for her father Arend and her only son, our Dad. Suddenly I understand why I could never be real close to Grandma Barb. She rather craved the affection of the men in the family after her mother departed. Was she trying to compensate them for Flora's desertion? Had Flora been part of a big family like ours, would she have been happy enough to stay? Did she go to the sisters in the Tasmanian cloister to have a big family?

I reread the last few pages and compare her version with others I've been given. Why did Tom Baudin say Flora spilled the beans after someone filled up her glass of sherry? She'd planned it all the day before!

And why did he say Flora wouldn't elope with him, if she says that he did not want her in his life? And which house in Queenscape did Arend own? And did Flora ever hear when Arend sold Sundew Cove? Flora, it seems, stayed at Sundew Cove until she left forever. Why did Tom not want to tell me about her return to Platypus, that one last time?

So many what ifs. Yet, I sense an important answer hidden somewhere in those last pages of my great-grandmother's diary, although it may take me half a lifetime to pin it down. I pull the curtain away from the window, switch off the light, push the diary under the mattress and watch the stars twinkle in an indigo sky. What an incredible universe this is. How stupid to fret over 'who-loves-me-who-loves-me-not' when there is so much to discover and such beauty to get high on. How can I sleep now?

But at dawn I wake from a deep sleep, knowing I dreamed without remembering what about. How I love the way the sun strikes through the window, dust particles dancing madly in a shaft that lights up corners. And the creaking of the wood when there is a southerly wind. And the stars in the sky when I lie here thinking sometimes late at night. Dawn is noisy. Birds, the rooster and a host of far-away mechanical noises testify that most people are up. I've slept in.

11: The Pact

The great clean-up has been accomplished. Coral and Zora now share my room, putting an end to reading at night. But I have more than enough to think about, so it doesn't matter.

The Crackmans have arrived and are settling in. Stephen is suddenly a head taller and looks down on me. Don't know how I feel about that. Don't know how I feel altogether about this new university student Stephen. Not only taller, with broader hands, but with a new manner. Or maybe not new, but borrowed from university mates – more than a bit affected. Maybe he behaves in this new way because he brought his friend Jason. The Crackmans apologised for having brought Stephen's friend unannounced, but it was decided at the last moment and he brought a blow-up mattress and sleeping-bag and will camp on the floor. Of course they're paying for him, so Mum said that was just fine.

Jason is like an arrow. Even when he stands still you feel the tension in him, ready to dart off as soon as he decides on the most remote, most exciting direction. He is the opposite of Stephen in every respect. Thin, lean, athletic, fast and smart and I guess a few years older. He laughs a lot, quickly and with shining eyes. Grey eyes. But he doesn't go on trying to get the most out of every laugh like Stephen, who has trouble raising humour.

Stephen and Jason will study in Canberra for different degrees, but plan to share a flat. So Mrs Crackman said she thought it a good idea if they did some domestic bonding during the holiday by sharing Stephen's room. Mr Crackman keeps aloof. His voice only mumbles and his tum rumbles as he reads piles of magazines in the verandah room.

I'm up before dawn these days, preparing guest breakfasts almost to the point of serving. Then I have to wait until Mrs Crackman comes through the connecting door and says: 'Bianka? Mr Crackman and I will have our breakfast now, please?' That means the guys have either gone for an early swim or are still asleep. Which means I cannot leave the kitchen until they get back or up. But I want to be outside in this beautiful weather too – talk to my seedlings, plant vegetable seeds, transplant the herbs and find wildflowers popping up.

I may feel annoyed, but remembering island hospitality I try to keep myself amused while hanging around the house. Mum and Auntie Branka are quilting and spinning today, so I have the place to myself except for the Crackmans. Next week the littlies have holidays too and the place will be buzzing. At the sewing machine I stitch up panels for my adventure suit and think.

I think about Jason. Something amazing has

happened. From the moment they arrived, and out of the blue, I felt attracted to Jason like a magnet, in a way I've never felt before with anyone. After a year of dreaming on and off about Stephen, this is a shock to the system. But I am floating like a feather on the wind. Stephen seems strange and out of reach. He has made no effort to talk to me alone, like we used to. I am sort of glad. I think we have grown dreadfully apart. I can't quite work out how that is possible after last summer on the rocks, when I was so close to telling him my secret dream. But maybe missing out on the kiss turned him off. If that is so, I'm glad I never did spill the beans, as Tom would say. My dream is still my dream. But I would like to tell it to Jason, whom I do not know at all. Yet, I feel he would understand. Is that what it is about? Sharing dreams with someone who says 'yeh, me too'?

But that is hardly likely. Jason is supposed to be bonding with Stephen. They go beachcombing together and neither Stephen nor Jason needs me for company. I just clean up after them. That doesn't hurt, really. But I would like to talk with Jason just once, to see what he is like. Meanwhile I sort of dream about him. It's very pleasant. At night I lie in bed looking at the stars, instead of reading and getting my head full of problems. I just daydream I'm talking to Jason until I fall sleep.

Knock on the door. 'Come in!' I get up from the sewing machine and it is Jason, tousle-haired, wrapped only in a white towel, doing a sort of crouching walk on bare feet. He was already tanned when he arrived and now the tan has a red glow. I feel a strange, strong cramp in my chest.

'Good morning! Pardon my costume. We had a wonderful swim to beat the sun to it, but it nearly froze the knobs off me.'

He's a character. Here is my chance. 'Did you see any seals?' I ask, to say something.

He straightens up, interest switched on. 'Do they come to your beach? I'd like to swim with them.'

'Don't,' I laugh. 'If they get annoyed they'll take a piece out of you, they're quite wild. They actually live further on, where the rocks give shelter. You can look down on their nursery from the cliff.'

Jason looks so intently at me that the grey of his eyes becomes like a sky in which I fly up. My hands do automatic things with breakfast food.

'Bianka, would you be my guide to the seals when you have time one day? Stephen isn't too keen on exploring, he prefers lazing about. But I want to take photographs to capture this island in all its facets.' So he's one of those postcard photographers!

'Sure,' I say, flipping over two eggs in the frypan. Me? Going exploring with Stephen's friend without Stephen? Is this really happening? Was Stephen never interested in exploring? Was he just dragged along by me? 'Do you want fried tomato, Jason?' Savouring his name.

'No! Please, no. And no bacon for me either. I eat vegetarian. I was going to ask for egg or cheese at dinnertime. Stephen has been eating my meat at dinner. Oh, I don't mind if my egg has kissed Stephen's bacon, as long as I don't have to eat it. But I'll have the tomato fresh if I may.'

Jason and I stand side by side at the kitchen bench fixing two breakfasts and when they are ready he leans over, gives me a quick peck on the cheek and picks up the plates, opening the door with his big toe, his towel slipping dangerously. 'See you later then!' he sings, winks, and the door falls shut behind his perfect shape.

I stand perplexed. Seventeen, never been kissed, and now in a split moment I've been kissed by Jason with the sky in his eyes. I touch my cheek, floating away on a happiness cloud. The hot water gushing from the tap seems to have new life in it, the view through the window has more intense colours, the sounds of birds and ducks out there is like a symphony! Quickly I clean utensils, wipe the bench and rush outside. I have to run. Feel the wind through my hair. Where to?

Ending up in the orchard I start weeding, in case any of the family should be looking for me. Then I remember they're all out, at school, at craft, in the paddocks. So I wander between the trees, seeing the pointy young leaves with new eyes, touching the swelling fruit buds.

Suddenly I feel another body right behind me, so close that I can feel its warmth. I freeze and turn, remembering Patrick Byderdike. Who else would sneak up on me like that? But two hands have already covered my eyes and I twist and struggle until Jason's voice says: 'Shoosh, you wild island girl. Don't be frightened. It's Jason the traveller, who didn't come to harm you!'

The hands move away and I turn to stare panting into Jason's laughing eyes. My heart pounds madly. Not from seeing him, but from adrenaline pumping as I prepared to defend myself. Suddenly I sink down in the grass and with face in hands I sob. I hear in great surprise how my voice heaves, first loud, then softer. Then it stops. I become aware of an arm around my shoulder and Jason's side pressed to mine. But he doesn't say a word. What must he think? How to explain?

I open my eyes and sniff and snort until my breath takes up its normal rhythm again. I turn to Jason and smile sheepishly. His eyes, always laughing, are now dark and concerned.

'I am so sorry!' he says in a voice that touches me to the core. 'That was very thoughtless of me. I should have realised … you live so isolated here … that was stupid and thoughtless of me, please forgive me.'

'No, no!' I stammer, wiping my face with the back of my hands, thinking that mainland girls must be used to being surprised like that all the time.

'Will you forgive me, please?' Jason asks. And without giving me time to reply: 'Shall we walk away a bit and talk a little?' his voice soft but urgent.

'Okay,' I say, 'but I have to tell you …' and make to stand up. Jason's hands move under my arms and we spring to our feet together in the grass. We are standing by the quince tree.

'What are these exquisite flowers?' Jason asks, holding a branch between two fingers. 'They are more delicate than the most perfect seashells. I've never seen such clear pale pink, like angels' wine.'

'They're quince flowers,' I tell him. 'They look fragile, but they produce tremendously large, knobbly fruit. Some people think quince tastes like fine wine.'

Jason looks at me. 'I shall call you Quince Flower.'

I just laugh. What to say? I like being a quince flower, they are my favourite spring blossoms.

'You were going to tell me something, Quince Flower?' he says, holding my hands, waiting.

'I thought you were …' and I tell him of the Byderdike incident and how I'd told Arend and what Dad had said on the phone to the fella.

Jason listens intently until I finish and says: 'No wonder!', folding me in his arms and stroking my hair. 'I must have given you the fright of your life and I only meant to surprise you. How totally thoughtless of me. I'm a stupid oaf.'

'No, no!' I protest, 'it isn't your fault!' I still feel simultaneously shocked and delighted. But how beautiful the world looks! My heart feels lighter then it has for ages. My feet seek the direction as we walk hand in hand towards the beach, crossing the new strip of land, straight for the cliff. The rollers boom against the rocks, the salt wind cuts our breath at the lips when we try to talk. We run, laugh and chase each other to the rocks.

We climb and because I am leading we climb all the way to the second cliff and then up to the cave where I always wanted to go. Beneath us young seals lie basking on the rocks.

'My cave,' I say, spreading my arms as if to invite Jason to my home. We sit down on damp stone slabs under the overhang, side by side, arms around our knees, looking out to sea.

'No land until Antarctica,' says Jason, awe in his voice.

'Except for Sometime Island,' I say.

'Sometime Island? Where is that?'

'It's not on the map. Only in my mind. It's my secret dream island and it must be somewhere out there in the ocean. When I feel really fed up with my life, I always imagine living like a hermit on Sometime Island.'

There. It is out. Jason is the first living human being to hear my secret. He is silent, but his face turns towards mine and his arm rests again around my shoulders. It is good. My secret is safe with him. At last he speaks.

'Girl, you really can fly. From the first moment I saw you I knew that you were not just a natural beauty. Can I ask you not to do something?'

I nod. I don't take advice very well, but with Jason it's different.

'Bianka, keep Sometime Island a secret. Keep it to yourself. Don't tell others. I'll keep it safe for you. And I want to say something about Stephen, too.'

I stiffen and he notices and his fingers start to rub my shoulder. 'Don't stiffen up. I've noticed how Stephen has been trying to avoid you and so I figured you and he were pretty close last holiday, is that right?'

'Not terribly close,' I reply, because closeness is what Jason and I have now. Not just his arm and our hands touching, but our minds honing in on each other like two bees from the same hive who've been separated by wind and weather for a long, long time. 'We were sort of friends and we walked and talked. That sort of thing. No more than that.'

Jason seems to be searching for words. 'Bianka, I like Stephen. He's a good bloke. We studied together for our foundation year and we will share a flat in Canberra, at least for starters. But he is a mother's boy and subconsciously he is looking for someone to take his mum's place. She knows it and she's hell scared he'll move in with some domineering girl before the first Canberra year is over. He may even think he ought to get married. That's why she is grooming me as brother's keeper. I don't mind. I'll talk him out of any mistakes he is likely to make until he gets stubborn. Then it's up to him. But you are too strong for Stephen. You'd be pulling and pushing him all the way. Don't fall for that.'

I'm sort of stunned. I partly recognise that what Jason says is true. But I hadn't come that far in my own thinking, let alone with Stephen. Feelings and emotions fight for supremacy in my chest until I blurt out: 'We were just friends. We were still school kids. And I am not the marrying kind.' I hear the echo of my words and nearly die. Here I sit with the most wonderful guy and I tell him I'm not the marrying kind! I must be crazy!

But Jason just chuckles and hugs me. 'Neither am I,' he hums. 'I've seen too many people make awful choices, including my own parents. So you and I are two of a kind. Do you think we could make a pact?'

'Yes!' I shout as my heart leaps up from the dungeons. All is right. The world is back together again. Jason and I are two of a kind! 'Yes! Let's make a pact!'

Down at the foot of the cliff the waves roll up and break, spouting foam that drapes like lace curtains over the black rocks. Sounds of sqealing seal pups. Smells of salt, wet sand, fish and kelp. These will always remind me of this morning when Jason and I sit in the cave working out our pact.

We are going to write to each other. Four times a year. It can be just a card saying 'Hello, I'm fine but wish you were here.' Or a long letter if we have something to tell that no one else will understand. Jason believes in the power of thought. If we have a real crisis of any sort, we must try to think so strongly of the other that we feel supported and can solve the crisis. Most important of all, we pledge to write to each other when we think we have found the right person to share our lives with. Then we must try to talk each other out of it to put our feelings to the test.

'And I want to write to you on your birthday,' I say, 'in case no one else does.' For I gather that Jason's family ties may not run to niceties like birthday cards and presents.

'Thank you, Quince Flower!' says Jason before he crawls deeper into the cave to find something to seal our pact on – a shell or a smooth stone. He crawls back with something long and thin hanging looped between his fingers.

'Look what I found. Someone has been here before us! There are remnants of a disintegrated hat lying back there.' He hands me a ribbon with the same pattern as the two from Flora's diary, even more worn and faded. 'This is rather perishable. We'd better pledge on a rock.'

'No,' I say. 'This ribbon has been here half a century. It will last for as long as our pact will last.' How did Flora's hat land in a south coast cave? Or was this ribbon the only kind for sale at Queenscape, so that all girls and women wore it? I will never know!

Jason looks sharply at me. 'How do you know? No, don't tell me, you woman of mysteries. The ribbon will be our link. Let's pledge and then I'll crawl back and put it where it has been lying for half a century, okay?'

What an amazing pact we make. What an incredible being, this Jason, whom I did not know a few days ago.

'Seal with a kiss,' says Jason and we meet in a kiss that makes the universe spin.

'Oh Bianka,' says Jason, holding me just so that we can look into each other's eyes. 'What a good thing we just made that pact. How can I ever forget it now?'

'And how could I?' I whisper, grinning from ear to ear.

We sit, side by side, arms around our knees again, wiggling our toes in our sneakers and looking out to sea and Sometime Island, which only we can see.

12: Connections

There aren't many more opportunities for Jason and me to talk, as the remainder of the Crackmans' holiday rolls off in a blaze of spring sunshine. They tour the island and Jason takes Stephen exploring – in the other direction of course. But every so often he is there, beside or behind me. He hums a tune when he comes up: 'Oh Quince Flower, Quince Flower, sing me a song …' so as not to scare me. So sweet. And he comes to collect breakfast for Stephen and himself every day now, under the pretext of making sure he gets vegetarian fare!

Even when Mum or the kids hover around we manage to snatch a conversation in half words and glances. 'You ought to think about going to university too, you know,' he whispers one day. 'You are starved for knowledge. Let me be your guide.' I nod, knowing he's right, but am only capable of living in the here and now. By the end of his holiday Jason and I will be like those twin stars you can see from our beach, far, far away beyond Sometime Island, twinkling and blinking in unison.

On the last morning we are alone in the kitchen for a few minutes. I give him a small envelope. Inside is the second ribbon from Flora's diary. 'Open it when you get home,' I tell him.

Jason gives me a folded piece of paper. 'My home

address,' he says. 'You'll get the Canberra one as soon as I find a place.' I open the paper and read 'Jason Jacobs. C/o School of Martial Arts' and the address in Adelaide and a date in January, his birthday.

'Martial arts!' I almost shout. 'That's what I want to do. Self-defence. How come you live there?'

'My sister and her husband run the school. It's a big building in the inner city. They live upstairs and I rent a room. They teach lots of courses. Do you really want to do martial arts? Yes, of course, I can see why ...' He becomes thoughtful again.

'I can pay my way,' I urge him. 'I have savings. But it has to be really intensive and short, like five days or so, because I can't afford somewhere to stay for much longer.'

'Leave it to me,' Jason says suddenly, with that decisiveness that makes me trust him so completely. 'I'll be in touch if I can stitch up a deal for you. Leave it to me, Quincey.' And he gives me a quick kiss while I disintegrate at the thought that someone will enter the kitchen just then.

The moment comes when they depart. Both families swap thank-yous and come-agains. Jason and I just look at each other and finally he formally shakes my hand, holding on for an extra squeeze, thanking me for my cooking while our eyes exchange a last message. I am vaguely aware that Stephen stands awkwardly by his mother's side. In the end I just smile at him and wave as I step backwards to the house. I stay there as long as I dare without attracting attention, to keep the invisible thread between Jason's mind and mine from snapping as the car drives out of sight. But it never breaks.

I must have been in a daze all day, because Dad comes to put his hand on my shoulder by evening. 'Tired, girl? You have done a great job looking after the visitors. Arend and I will shift the littlies straight back where they belong tonight, so you can have your room to yourself again.'

I look at him tenderly, really grateful. 'Thanks, lovely Dad,' I say and peck him on the cheek. He smiles, a bit surprised, and calls Arend. I haven't been so affectionate for a long while.

Now I lie in bed, looking at the stars. What an amazing turn my life has taken. Nothing has changed in the day-to-day pattern, nor do I have a plan for my future. Yet everything looks different. When the news on the radio tonight mentioned Canberra, my heart flipped. I'll be having a lot of heart flips next year just on account of news from Canberra, where my pact partner will be.

My thoughts turn to Flora. It was she that made me say: 'I'm not the marrying kind.' Sometimes I don't quite know whether I speak my own thoughts or Flora's. But I am more and more convinced that she and I are closer than any two people in our family that I know of. She with her dream island, leaving her hat with that ribbon in the cave. She must have ridden her horse from the north coast before leaving Platypus, to say goodbye to her dream island. Or just to sit in bliss, as she would say. If I never find anything again that belonged to her, I've found enough. Because in some inexplicable way she has become my role model after all. Not that our lives are the same or mine will become like hers – never, never – but almost as if my life is a continuation of hers by natural selection. Her life story tells me how to avoid those miscalculations – her word – that made her existence on Platypus Island impossible.

I sleep. I dream. I walk on rocks with a spring in my step, holding hands. I can't see Jason, but it must be him I'm holding hands with. I walk until I just hold the ribbon. I wake up and the sun dances through the dust to the far corner where the wood creaks. There is a strong southerly today and the verandah rattles a little tune. I miss Jason something awful.

It being Saturday, everyone flies off in all directions. But before we separate after breakfast, Dad calls us all together.

This afternoon,' he says, 'after soccer, I would like to call a family conference. Big changes afoot. Nothing bad. It could be very good, even exciting. I won't say more now, but I would like you all to be here. We are going to discuss our future on this farm.'

'Us too?' asks Yvan, used to being free of such duties as one of the littlies.

'Yes, you and Zora and Coral, the whole family.'

Surprise, surprise. What is Dad up to? That dashes any plans I might have had to ring Sylvie. But now that I don't need to poke Flora's diary back behind the brick there's no urgency. And I don't want to talk about Jason to anyone. Perhaps I should go and see Tom Baudin. I have a few more questions for that old salty beard.

'Can I have Whoopsy this morning?' I ask around. Arend nods, Coral nods. I wipe the kitchen surfaces and hurry the kids on to make their beds. I tell Mum there's heaps of things for a great stir-fry in my plots: swedes, bok choy, radish, carrot, spring onion and coriander. And fish in the freezer.

'I'll cook rice in bed then, and make a fresh fruit salad,' she says, 'if you do the stir-fry.' Mum's way of cooking rice comes from the old country, where they used hay boxes. She brings the rice to the boil until the water has evaporated, wraps the pot in newspapers, rushes to the bed, pops it in the middle and covers it with blankets and pillows. Cooks to perfection in a few hours.

'That's fixed then,' I say and go to my room to put on warmer clothes. Whoopsy is pleased to go riding. She hasn't had many outings lately, everyone being so busy. We clip-clop along the drive to the road, for I'm taking the official route today. There are quite a few cars about. All smells change here. Petrol fumes dominate. Visitors in hired cars. Day people. The season is building up. I hope we'll get another booking.

That makes me think of Jason. Everything makes me think of Jason. I mustn't write before Christmas, but I write letters in my mind, tell him what I'm doing. I plan a special birthday card for the sixteenth of January. We are connected, I feel it every waking moment. I'm happy and much more relaxed. I don't worry about my future any more. Jason and I talked of how we want to live. We agreed on the essentials and I know them by heart:

– We have to concentrate on our own talents and what we love doing best.

– We have to follow up where that can lead us.

– When we know our direction we must go for it, organise for it, move for it if necessary, work for it and study for it until we achieve it.

– We must live as independently as possible to avoid getting distracted from our goal.

– Everything we do should be good for something. For people, the environment, the world.

– We will help each other wherever we can.

It's pretty simple really. Each idea gives rise to another, that's why it's so easy to remember. Jason told me how undecided he'd been after leaving school. He went to work for a couple of years, first in a department store, then as brickie's labourer and finally as a waiter in a posh restaurant. He learnt about life and other people and what he likes and dislikes. Then he went to university to do a foundation course in the humanities and finally realised he wants to write full-time, eventually. He will also do Pacific Studies, because that's his great interest. He has been to Fiji and Tonga already. I think he likes islands.

'Did you know it was because of Charles Dickens' novels that they closed down those terrible work-houses in England, where kids as young as ten were starved and bullied? Today the world has other problems; I've been a lone crusader sometimes but I feel so powerless. Through writing I can perhaps influence people and it is what I do best.' He already has poems and articles published, is working on a novel and a book about student environmental activism. He says he won't send me any poems because they aren't as good as he thinks they should be, but one day he'll write one specially for me.

I told Jason I wasn't ready to decide whether I want to go to university, but maybe in a year's time I could be. I am still in an undecided stage. He said things would become clear soon enough, because I have a mind that never stops ticking. Nobody else would ever have noticed that about me. He said he'd look up university courses for remote students for me on the net. 'Something to do with botany,' I said.

I reach the turn-off for Tom Baudin's cliff. The lone petrol station and deli of Pa Makeshore on the corner, a few houses, a horse and a cow, then just track and field. Whoopsy is in her element. She can smell the sea and goes for it. But today there's no time to trot through the waves. Tom's cliff looms up bigger and darker than I remember it. Just for the exercise we gallop the last kilometre.

At the foot of the cliff are two sturdy rails and I tie Whoopsy to the one where fresh grass grows between the rocks. 'Won't be long, Whoopsy.' I pat her on the rump and begin the climb. Tom is outside his cabin and hears pebbles rolling from under my feet. He stops what he is doing and stands there, knees and arms half bent, watching. I guess his eyesight isn't the best. When I get to his little plateau he begins to smile.

'Hello Mr. Baudin, it's Bianka.'

'Ah, you are John's girl. How nice of you to come and visit me.'

Has he forgotten our last conversation? He opens the door wide and we step in. The usual ordered chaos. He carries a billy in his hand. 'Just making tea,' he says as if that is a rather amazing coincidence.

Soon we sit on the only two chairs with mugs of black tea. He's out of milk. I offer to go Pa Makeshore on Whoopsy and get him some, but he says he'll take the jeep down later to Queenscape for supplies.

'How's your father?' Tom asks. 'And dear Tinka and Branka?' I tell him they are well and then remember some stories of Arend and the kids that may interest him. I also tell him we had visitors for ten days, without going into detail. 'They come every year,' I say. He nods, eyes and mind drifting off. I decide to make a move.

'Remember, Mr. Baudin, how we talked about Flora Hammermeyer last time? My great-grandmother?'

The same stunned look and expression of shock before he collects himself. 'Ah, Flora, the Goddess of Flowers,' he sighs, just like last time.

'Yes,' I say, barely concealing my impatience. I did not come to hear endearments he may have spoken to Flora fifty years ago. They ring rather hollow now, considering what she wrote in her diary.

'You said you'd tell me about the last time she came back to Platypus, remember?'

He startles a little, but pulls himself together once more. 'Nothing much to tell,' he says, withdrawing into his shell. 'She came back to arrange affairs for the children. She didn't wear the habit, but she was almost unrecognisable. Not a lick of cream on her face, hair under a scarf, probably shaven off. Black clothes and stockings and shoes.'

'What habit?' I ask. She must have said goodbye to the cave before that visit.

'She joined the Sisters of Mercy to Little Birds in Tassie. I only saw her for a moment as the boat arrived. I didn't know she was coming. Nobody knew. It was just coincidence. We only exchanged greetings. She left inside a week and was never heard of again.'

I could see him scrambling off to avoid her, embarrassed, feeling guilty. He could not know she had finally chosen what she really wanted to be and do.

'She could still be alive then?' I ask with mounting excitement.

'Oh no. She died long before Arend did. He got the notice. Around the time your mum and dad were married.'

It's a blow. Flora has become such a reality for me that the news of her death makes my heart sink. But I must ask the other vital question, just as if I were doing an oral history project.

'Mr. Baudin, you told me she wouldn't elope with you. But do you know why she wouldn't, since she had your son?'

Again he is visibly rocked by my question. He may think me intrusive. He isn't getting into a flow like last time. He opens his mouth a few times until an answer comes out.

'Elope. Well, we wouldn't have been able to elope very far. From one end of the island to the other. She wanted to leave altogether, but that was not possible.'

'Why not?' I lower my voice so as not to stop his thought processes.

'Not possible. I couldn't go back to the mainland. Not welcome there. And I could not provide for her and the boy here. I'm only a possessionless hermit. Always have been. I told her she'd be better off where she was.' He gets up to grab the kettle to refill his mug, then finds it emptying. 'No more tea,' he says. It could be a hint.

'I'm just about to leave anyway,' I assure him. 'I

brought you radishes from my garden. I grew them myself.' I pull the bunch of bright red little globes with their tufts of green leaves from my shoulderbag and put them on the table. He looks at them as if he hasn't seen radishes in years. Maybe he hasn't, living on fish, bread and tea as he does.

'Thanks for the cuppa,' I say, getting up. 'Nice talking to you again.'

'Yes, yes,' he mumbles and walks me to the door. I wave before I clamber down. He waves back, stooped with age, burdened with memories. I feel a bit sorry for him, having raked up old times for my own satisfaction. But somehow they are part of my times too. And then, I reckon he'll soon forget and dream again of Flora Goddess of Flowers, as he has done for half a century to deaden his own sense of failure.

Looking at the position of the sun, I figure Whoopsy and I have time for a quick run through the waves. She whinnies when she sees me and soon we race into the wind along the beach, splashing up foam in the shallows as the tide goes out. Inhaling deeply, I bob up and down in the saddle. We spin around where the cliff juts out in the sea and run back, before we slow down to trot up the track through the fields again.

So old Tom wasn't really prepared to elope with the love of his life. Before Barbara came along, Flora would have followed him with Frederik if only he'd been prepared to leave the island. Not welcome on the mainland. Did he have a criminal past? Or life-long enemies from courting other men's girlfriends? Was Flora irritated with Barbara because her own loyalty as a mother made any reconciliation with Tom impossible after the birth of Arend's daughter?

Whatever the case, Tom protected himself very nicely, holding on to his comfortable isolation. He never loved her as much as he wants to believe he did. His dramatic talk is just empty theatrics. And what about not being able to provide for Flora and Frederik because he was a poor hermit? Last time he said he'd earned enough money to buy Sundew Cove! He's a bit of a liar as well, old Tom is.

I am coming to terms with Flora dying before I was born. She seems to have followed her own bliss, did at last what she should have done in the first place, before she had children. She could have become an independent artist then, a bohemian. Having kids makes everything difficult. Barbara was a bit young to lose her mother to a nunnery, even though she was at boarding school.

Yet, the connection between Flora and me is getting stronger. I feel her longing for a life of her own in my fibres, in my mind. One day I will paint the birds of Platypus, with the plants they feed on. I am no longer alone with my thoughts, hopes and desires. There were Flora's before mine, and now there are Jason's to link up with in the future.

13: The Great Make-Over

Auntie Branka brings new knitting as I wheel her into the livingroom for the family conference. Handspun socks for Dad. He swears none wear better in rubber boots. Mum has outdone herself with a lemon cake on the table and the kettle on the boil. Everyone is here and Dad wastes no time.

'I know you kids must be mighty curious to hear what all this is about. Well, Arend and Auntie Branka and Mum and I have done quite a bit of figuring and discussing of late and today it's your turn. Arend has made me see that ever since ancient times farms never were factories producing just one or two commodities for sale. We think the days of farming wool and wheat for good profits may well be over forever. For decades now the farm is always just scratching by, never making quite enough to get ahead. And since wool prices can never be depended on, we'll have to get off the sheep's back.

'The government blokes say 'get bigger or get out', the banks will lend us money until they own us, but we think they have no right to tell people to leave farms that have been the family home for generations. If we sold this place to become a holiday resort, we would scarcely be able to buy a house in town and then what would we do for a living? On the other hand, the farm is feeding us well, we don't lack in the essentials. We have meat, eggs, fruit, vegetables, honey, cheese and get our own flour milled. The only difficulty is earning cash for equipment, rates and taxes. On top of that you're all growing up, needing clothes and things for school or to give you a start in life, not to mention health insurance and things like that.'

Here Dad seems a bit vague and everyone tries not to look at Mum who cost a lot last year, but I wait with interest for what is to come, without being able to see how it can affect me right now.

'It started with Arend telling me he wants to become a full partner in the farm. That pleases me very much, for he and I get a lot of work done together and my working life has become much more bearable since Arend came into it. I said to him that to be fair I had to think of all of you. Maybe Bianka wants to become a share farmer too and later on there's Coral and Yvan and Zora.'

'Dad, that never occurred to me,' I interrupt. 'I would have told you last year if that's what I'd wanted.'

'So you don't want to be a farmer, that's okay. But then I got this idea in my head. We must find ways so that any one of you who doesn't want to leave home in the years to come, can become a working partner in the farm. That means looking at the farm as more than just a wheat and wool producer. The whole farm must become our first source of livelihood. By that I mean we must grow things that benefit us as a family directly, not via a wool board or a wheat board or any other agency that takes a cut before we get a cheque. And Arend has come up with some proposals.'

I'm getting interested. I like the idea of becoming a full partner in the farm, but what can I do? 'You mean self-sufficiency farming, Dad?' Dad nods in Arend's direction, who clears his throat for a speech. He seems pretty excited.

'I want to stay on the farm,' Arend says, 'because I'm pretty well plugged in here. So I have to justify my living here. This farm used to be just sheep and wheat, but that doesn't pay its way any more. Thanks to Dad making do for years, we aren't in debt except for paying off the cheese room and equipment. So Dad and I talked about diversifying more than we do already and we discussed adding value to our products and selling more or most of it direct. For starters, that didn't seem possible without capital. You want a leg-up to get to the point where you can do things the simple way and reap a direct profit.'

Dad cuts in: 'Here I must pay tribute and I want you all to know that Auntie Branka has come to the rescue. She enabled us to buy the new strip of land recently and is now a full partner in the farm. Why is that land so important? For two reasons. Firstly, to prevent anyone else doing something there that disturbs the peace or pollutes our land. You never know what these mainlanders come up with next. Holiday cabins or worse. Secondly, it's important for our paying guests to have direct beach access. Because we want to talk with all of you about taking bookings right through the year. And getting a photo of the homestead into the Island Holidays brochure and on the internet.'

My heart sinks. More visitors? Will I never be able to get out of the kitchen and laundry? And much as I love the girls, I don't want to share my room all year round!

Auntie Branka says: 'It's an investment. And I am prepared to make a few more outlays to get this farm productive for every one of you. There is no better investment than land. Gold and silver can lose value, shares tumble, but land is solid.'

Arend guffaws and says that some farmers believe the opposite, usually after they've ruined their land by overclearing, overgrazing or overcropping. 'They are wrong both ways,' declares Auntie Branka with her usual conviction.

'Now I dont want you to think,' Dad resumes, 'that more visitors is going to mean Bianka wearing herself thin running after them. She has done a stirling job this year, but she may want to do other things with her life, so from now on we will all pick up part of the load, because we all benefit.

'For starters, Arend and I will do all the shifting of beds and belongings. It's too heavy for Mum, and Bianka shouldn't be doing it alone. We will also mop the rooms before and after and when necessary. But we sort of wondered whether one of you girls would like to do a course in fine cooking? You know, with them sprigs of greenery and coloured sauce on a plate?'

We all turn to Coral, who jumps up. 'I've told you before, Dad, I want to be a gourmet cook. Bianka doesn't want to. I do, I do. Can I leave school?'

'No!' says Mum and that is that. Coral sinks down.

Dad looks worried. 'Coral, we're doing long-term planning here. No cock-a-hoop harebrained schemes we may regret later. You have to finish at least Year Eleven – that's only fourteen months to go. Then you can do a cooking course or apprenticeship, perhaps in the Sea & Salt. After that you can become head cook at the Woodsman's Homestead straight away, or be a cook somewhere else if we can't pay enough. But you can do as much cooking as you like in the holidays, isn't that so, Bianka?'

I brighten up. 'Sure!' I say. 'As long as I'm in charge of growing the fruit and vegies, I'm happy!'

'And Yvan,' Dad says, 'you could be a great help pitching in with running and storing supplies. It's men's work. Too heavy for Bianka and Tinka.'

Yvan, who always tries to get out of things, flexes his biceps and lets Arend test how hard they are. 'You'll do fine, matie,' says Arend. 'We must exercise your muscles a bit more on the farm too.'

'And what can I do?' pipes up Zora. Such a doll.

Look at her round face turned up at Dad as if she expects a present.

'Now Zora, my love, in the coming year you have to see to it that the workers get their refreshments on time and take a rest. You cut the cake, put it on plates, and make tea and coffee or cordial for everyone. You tell them to sit down and take a rest. If somebody doesn't look after the workers, the whole plan will fail.'

The poor kid will have to pitch in straight after school. But Zora looks suitably impressed with her new position. 'Can I start now?' she asks. Mum pushes cake and knife towards her and she begins to cut slices and share them around. 'Time everybody takes a break,' Zora announces and we all chuckle.

'We'll ease into the visitors bookings to find our level,' says Dad. 'I don't want anybody getting stressed out. So by the time Coral leaves school we should know where we are with that. And if Bianka or Coral should want to leave home one day to do something else, hopefully we will have built up enough income to hire someone else to cook.' Wow! He's thinking big!

'Any ideas about this?' asks Dad. 'Before we get on to farm products?'

I still can't think of anything to ask and don't dare to bring up the room issue. Can't see where I come in, except with what I do already. 'So for the time being I keep growing the vegetables and cooking the meals?' I ask, just to show interest, wishing I had a plan of my own to put forward.

Dad says: 'Mum has noticed you get rather tired on washing days. So Arend ... go ahead, son.'

Arend smiles a wicked smile. 'This is a huge sacrifice I'm making, sis!'

I'm annoyed. 'So what about my sacrifices?'

'I'll match you. How would it be if you and I did the washing together? You load and I hang it out? Together we should do it in no time if we start early. I want to start building or farm work at eight. So you and Mum still have to bring it in.'

'Wow, brother,' I say. 'I'm impressed! And I accept. You start tomorrow! And remember, when we have guests we run the washing machine five times a week, not three!'

'Done!' says my brother. Life is looking up.

'And about the cooking,' says Dad, 'Tinka?'

'I was just coming to it,' says Mum. 'I think I can take charge of the meals again in normal times, if Bianka or Coral pitch in when we have guests. And I'd really like to go back to the cheese room. Arend has done well with the cheese this year, but with beehives and building, supplies and washing and cleaning, his time is limited. It needs one person to be in control of the turning, checking and keeping the temperature constant. I always liked making cheese. And when I feel I'm coping well again I want to make yoghurt. That needs a bit of extra equipment, not a lot.'

'You want to take over the milking too, Mum?' asks Arend cheekily. Dad throws him a look.

'Don't you overdo things, Tinka,' says Dad. 'No doubt yoghurt will sell. Bert Pronk told me the other day his uncle is exporting sheep yoghurt to the mainland and can't keep up with demand. But easy does it, Tinka, making it just for us will be fine.'

I am amazed at being released from being head cook. Freedom at last!

'Can I learn to drive?' asks Yvan, 'to get the supplies?' Anything technical gets him in.

'No harm here on the property,' says Arend. 'Under supervision. I'll teach you. But you have to wait a few years before hitting the road.'

'I just want to learn driving the truck,' laughs Yvan. He's always pretty insistent on fringe benefits for his own clever self.

'Let's talk about the farm,' says Dad. 'Arend and I have been investigating some possibilities – he'll talk first.'

Arend feels important, you can tell. He clears his throat again. 'I've looked at a few books,' he announces. 'We must improve our cash income, but it is just as important to produce more for our own use, so that we reduce our spending. We may look into different grains and I want to experiment with legumes. But in the first place we are looking at planting wood lots for timber along the north and east boundary – for our own use and for sale. That's long-term, but it doesn't cost much. We'll collect the seed off the trees this spring and germinate them. Then we shift one fence. A couple of planting picnics in winter and that's one project completed.'

'We plant trees at school every year,' says Zora. 'I have planted a wattle and a pink gum and they are already this high.' She holds her hand to her chin.

'I dig holes for the girls at school,' says Yvan, looking annoyed when Arend bursts out laughing before continuing.

'Now, about the cheese room. That's been going four years and because of buying equipment we haven't turned a real profit yet, but sales have steadily increased. So Dad and I thought we should keep more new lambs for cheese production, although we'll want to reduce stock overall. But we'll still shear quite a bit of wool and Yvan should learn to become the rousabout next shearing.'

'Wool! That's where I come in!' shouts Auntie Branka triumphantly.

'You were in there from the start, Branka,' says Dad, 'but let Arend tell you about the shop.'

'What shop?' 'Which shop?' 'Who's shop?' 'Our shop?' We all talk at once.

'We're going to built a shop by the road, at the gate,' says Arend, a wide grin on his face. 'As a matter of fact we are going to built a house for me, with a shop attached, and I'm going to live there. We can sell lots of things in the shop, but mainly our own produce: honey, cheese and anything else we make or have surplus of. How would you like to run the shop for an afternoon in the school holidays, Coral?'

'I'd love it,' says Coral. 'Can we sell cakes and coffee too?'

'That's my department,' cries Zora.

'Okay, so you can come and do the serving,' Coral argues back, 'but I'm in charge!'

'Hey girls, you're so fast,' says Arend. 'These are great ideas. Let's try it out in the peak season. But I wanted to tell you about how we're going to build the house, Dad and me.'

'Who's going to run the shop?' I ask. A silence follows. Dad and Arend look at me and Mum.

'I can't sit in a shop all day waiting for customers if I'm growing fruit and vegetables, gathering eggs, helping with meals, doing the washing and ironing ...' I take a breath. 'Don't get me wrong, I think the shop could be a great thing for us, but what if I want to do a full-time course or something, like we talked about?'

'We will take turns!' Auntie Branka says, always positive. 'And I will take the lion's share because I cannot move around much anyway.'

'We'll make a roster,' says Mum, 'so we can choose times that suit Branka, and Bianka if she's here, and myself with Coral. Yvan and Zora in the holidays. You will serve in the shop some afternoons, won't you kids?'

'I'd love it,' says Coral. 'Can I be in charge of the shop then?'

'Hey girls,' Arend tries again, 'let me tell you

about how Dad and I figured we're going to build the house and shop. We're going to build the whole place ourselves!'

We fall silent. Island men built lots of things, but a whole house and a shop?

'Mud bricks!' shouts Dad. He glows as if he invented them. 'Plenty of mud in the dam. It needs scooping out and widening anyway. Arend and I checked building magazines in the library and it's easy. We went and talked to Larry Brock who built a holiday chalet with mud bricks. So we made a couple of moulds and did an experiment to convince the council.'

'That's how you got so muddy the other day!' I remember.

'That's right. We were making mud pies!'

'I'll be in that!' shouts Yvan.

'Me too!' cries Zora.

'Yuck, leave me out,' says Coral.

'Why don't you all make mud bricks in the nuddy,' I say. 'Or we'll never get through washing days.'

'We're getting better,' Arend protests. 'We have one row of bricks already drying out. They're shaping up beautifully. The whole building is going to be made of cost-free mud bricks, so we'll only have to buy roofing and fittings. We'll get secondhand windows and doors and make a bush verandah with tree trunks. You'll see, it's going to look fantastic!'

Arend looks so proud and happy getting a place of

his own. I bet he's thinking of having a wife one day. She'd better like running a shop! If only I could have a place of my own.

'And then,' says Dad, 'we went to the council and talked around and got some lists of light industries they think would do well here on Platypus. Things that are sustainable, that won't run out of raw materials. Apart from what we've already mentioned, they'd like to see more eucalyptus oil production. But you need another set of equipment for that, so we've shelved it for the time being. Then there's apricots ...'

I drift off. Thinking about a place of my own, however small. A hut will do. A hermit's hut, with a bed, a chair and a tea kettle. Like Tom's place.

Dad's voice drones on. 'They seem to think seed-collecting could be a growth industry on these islands, for botanical gardens, nurseries and revegetation schemes. We have good stands of many species on the farm, so maybe we could look into that. It doesn't cost much to start off.'

Seed-collecting? 'Hey Dad, do you mean collecting seed from our native shrubs and trees? I can do that! That's what I want to do! I know all the species!' That's a blatant lie, but I read the books, I can look them up. 'And I can collect wattle-seed. The edible kind, non-toxic. It sells at twenty dollars a kilo for baking bread and biscuits and they make a sort of coffee from it.'

'We could bake wattle-seed bread and biscuits for

ourselves and the guests and the shop,' says Mum, 'so as not to deplete the trees.'

'I rather thought you might be interested, Bianka,' says Dad. 'You need a seed-collecting licence from the council if you collect outside the property, but you can start on the farm. We could make the shed lean-to fit for storage. We'll just enclose the open side and put a door in.'

Arend butts in. 'Dad, don't forget we were also going to ask Bianka to grow our tree seedlings for the woodlot.'

'I have a much better idea, Dad,' I cut in, all fired up. 'I will set up seedboxes for trees in the vegie garden, on a trestle table.' I am so excited, the words suddenly tumble out. 'And I also want to build a house of my own. On the new strip of land. A two-room mudbrick hut. One will be the seed room, and the other for me to live in.' I see it all before me in full form and colour. I will live with the sound of the breakers, within cooee of my cave.

Everyone seems stunned. I have taken my leap out of stagnation. This is what I really want to do. This is how I want to live at least next year. Building, growing trees and seed-collecting. Nothing is going to stop me. I will go for it, organise for it, move towards it, work for it, study for it – until I achieve it. Jason, partner, I've broken through the confusion!

14: Girls Can Build Houses

When I come down to earth I see all the familiar faces focused on mine. 'Are you going to build your own house?' asks Zora in awe. 'Can girls do that?'

'Yes. Girls can build houses. I will accept a little bit of help,' I grin, 'but I'm going to make my own mud bricks, even if it takes a year. And I stay in charge of the vegetable garden as well, and the orchard and the chooks, because that's what I'm best at. As long as I get early starts in the morning without you kids holding me up, I could have my hut up before winter.'

'Can I have your room then, Bianka?' Zora pleads.

'Sure, sis.' I stroke her glossy hair. She'll love waking up in my creaky room.

'And Yvan can have my room when I move into my house,' says Arend. 'That leaves only Coral to be shifted when visitors come.'

'But I like my room!' protests Yvan. 'I want to stay there.'

'You can't if we get year-round bookings, buddy,' says Dad and instantly Yvan sulks.

'And I want to have the computer in my room next year, because Yvan's room is always a mess,' complains Coral.

'But then he has to use it in your room,' Mum decrees. 'It's everyone's computer and I want no fights over it.'

'Why don't we,' says Dad, 'leave it with Yvan for

the time being, but shift it so we don't have to step over his stuff. And Yvan has to keep the computer table and chair free of junk. That alright, Yvan?'

'Sure,' says Yvan. 'I'm not *that* messy.' Laughter, as Yvan gets ribbed over his habits.

'You can stay in that room if you do your shifting all by yourself every time we have visitors,' says Arend. Yvan groans. He can't get out of this one.

'I don't know whether the council will give permission for a third house on the property,' says Dad, looking worried. 'What with electricity and plumbing.'

Instantly I'm in fighting mode. 'I don't want electricity. An oil or gaslamp will do, or candles. I'll have a rainwater tank, and an old sink. I can come to the house for a shower or take a dip in the sea. And if the council doesn't want to see farming families walk off their land and kids leaving the island after school, they have to be realistic. If we are to be full partners in the farm and doing a job, or building up some small industry on the family farm, then we have to live on the farm, don't we? My hut will be half business space anyway. I am sure they will see reason.'

'She's right,' says Arend. 'They can't suggest diversifying without allowing a few extra buildings. We can't do everything in the woolshed. They had no objection to us adding the cheese room and they're sure to understand that a seed room has to be separate too. We should simply apply for a licence to build storage and office for the seed business, and if need be we go and argue for it.'

'Thanks,' I say to my brother. He can be a great ally and he is learning the ropes.

'Well,' says Auntie Branka. 'Such big plans. After this nobody will be interested in what I have to offer the family partnership.'

'Without you we couldn't have new plans,' says Dad.

I walk around the table to hug her because I love her and she looks a little defeated. All our wild plans have left her behind in her wheelchair. And I'm even demanding they let me live on the land she financed. 'Auntie Bee, I'll still be here in the house every day to talk with you!'

'I know you will, my heart. But I also have something that I like doing very much. Your dad always says there's nothing better to wear in work boots than handspun, handknitted socks. And I love to spin and knit. We will get a shop. I want to make socks. Everyone makes jumpers, beanies and scarves, more than they can sell. But knitting socks is becoming a lost art. And they wear out sooner than beanies, you know! People need two pairs to start with and a new pair every six months. That's a growth industry! And from our own Romney fleeces! Farmers, fishermen, shearers, road workers, guides and rangers, researchers, sports people, they all need pure wool socks. I'll make publicity by advertising in the *Argus*. And I will sit in the shop and knit!'

'Wow,' I say. Mum is smiling, at last. Arend looks pleased. The littlies are wriggling, they want to go outside.

'More tea anyone?' asks Mum.

'That's my job,' says Zora. 'More tea anyone?'

'Wouldn't mind a fresh cuppa, puppet,' Dad says. 'Just make another pot, I'm sure it will be drained.' Zora steps deftly to the kitchen bench with the teapot, empties it in the compost bucket in the cupboard and fills the jug. I watch her doing what she must have watched others doing for years.

'I would like to try selling my quilts,' says Mum. 'I've just about finished the last one for the guest beds. Then I'd like to make cot quilts with native animal designs and hang them in the shop. If I price them reasonably, they'll sell to tourists. I've collected enough fabrics to keep me going for years and for filling I want to try teased wool fleece.'

'You're welcome to a bale of the best,' says Dad. 'What else can you make out of fleece, ladies? I'm open to any new ideas!'

'Well,' Mum says in her careful way, 'I was thinking of putting up a sign, maybe an advertisement saying: "Want a heritage quilt, or a copy of your lost childhood quilt? Katinka can make it." It would be a real challenge to get a commission.'

'What a wish fest,' I laugh. 'I can just see Mum's heritage quilts taking off. Maybe we will all end up doing what we really love to do.'

'That's the whole idea!' shouts Dad. 'This is no longer about maximum output per acre and bleeding the soil to death! This is about our lifestyle! It's about what keeps us healthy and what makes us happy. I warn you now, by the end of next year we may not have any more money in the bank, perhaps even less, and you will have worked harder for sure, but we should be living more interesting lives! And more choice for you kids.'

'Hear, hear,' Auntie Branka shouts, as they do in parliament.

'Here comes the tea,' says Zora, carrying the pot on a tray and placing it shakily on the table. Is she not too small for this job? But she's growing up fast. She'll rise to it. Such a simple thing, but a huge responsibility for her and she wants to do it, the sweetie.

'Can we go now?' asks Yvan, pushing his chair back. He's afraid he'll end up with an apprenticeship in the cheese room!

'Just a minute,' says Dad. 'There's one more thing we must discuss with all of us. The apricot trees. Evidently there is a demand for late-season apricots and because we are so far south they'll ripen late enough here. Personally I can see difficulties with export of soft fruit to the mainland, but the demand is equally strong for dried and preserved apricots. That's where we definitely come in. But it takes group effort to harvest and process the fruit.'

All of us remember how last autumn our fruit lay

rotting on the ground, because Mum was too weak to preserve it and I didn't know how to do it. 'I read in the *Argus* about sun-dried fruit without chemicals,' I say, before Dad puts his plan on the table.

'Correct,' he says. 'That's the way to go. I thought we should plant twenty apricot trees and come first harvest time in two years, we divide into two teams, because they ripen all at once. Arend, Yvan and I will be picking the fruit, and Tinka, Bianka and Coral organise the preserving.'

'Twenty trees!' I gasp, thinking I may not even be here in two years' time. 'How many jars do you think we can sell? Even if we manage to preserve apricots full pelt for two weeks without getting so sick of them that we go on strike?'

'Yep. About two weeks. Very short and very sweet, seeing we have fifty-two weeks in the year,' quips Dad.

'No, no,' says Mum, 'we'll sort them. The best ones go whole into jars, for ourselves, the visitors and the shop. With the medium ones we take out the stones and dry them. The rest go into the pot for jam. But by the time the trees are mature, I hope we can sell them fresh as well.'

'Apricot chutney,' says Coral. 'Yummmm!'

'Apricot chutney? Never seen it,' I tease her.

'I have. On the net. You stew apricots with sugar and onions and cloves and lemon rind …'

'Apricots with onions? Yuck!' spits Yvan.

'I tell you,' Coral addresses me and Mum, ignoring her younger brother, 'that a first-class country style homestead doesn't just serve visitors homemade cakes. You have to offer *nouvelle cuisine*. That means your own marmalades, pickles, preserves and chutneys and they have to taste like nowhere else. Then people keep coming back to buy jars for presents and impressing their friends.'

'Coral,' says Dad, 'you are going to be the hostess with the mostest, I see that coming. You'd better be in charge of collecting recipes then.'

'I have lots already,' says Coral, 'and if you give me money for a ringbinder with plastic pockets, I'll fill it up with gourmet recipes. Alphabetically.'

'Done,' says Dad, reaching in his vest pocket and handing Coral five gold coins. 'That enough, pet?' She nods, pleased.

Yvan wrinkles his forehead trying to think how he can come up with a scheme that yields an expense account. But he hasn't done the spadework like Coral has and sinks backs on his chair, bored.

'Excellent,' says Arend. 'Let's discuss a timetable. Our team will have to pick all the ripe fruit of half the trees, the other half a couple of days later. Apricots can ripen all in one week. Mum's team processes the first lot before we pick again. We could be done in two weeks if the weather is right, couldn't we?'

'Depending on whether we're hosting guests or not,' I protest. I like the idea, everyone likes apricots, but boy, the work and the mess! 'And everybody should keep their own rooms clean from now on or we'll never do it all.'

'Agreed,' says Dad and not even Yvan dares to protest.

'So,' says Auntie Branka. 'Two teams. So! Well, I'll be a one-woman team then, sitting at this table, taking out the kernels, writing the labels, sticking them on and putting cotton bonnets on the jars for the shop.'

'You're a trooper, Branka,' says Dad. 'What can I say to a family that's so keen on slave labour?' He spreads his arms as wide as they will stretch.

'Can I suggest,' I put up my hand, 'that you buy ten early trees and ten late varieties? So we preservers can have a break of it?'

'That's a sound idea, Bianka. We'll look into that. It's rather late to plant fruit trees now, but Arend and I have decided to go ahead anyway and water them through summer from a tank on the truck. We'll order them Monday and get the end-of-season discount!'

'A year's extra growth,' says Arend. 'Next year on drippers. We must put another ten-thousand-gallon tank on the shed.'

'Now, you youngsters may be excused,' Dad announces, 'unless you have any more questions?'

Yvan pushes back his chair and is out the door before anyone can stop him. He's in need of a romp and a ball game with Dreadlocks. Coral goes off to her room for teenage business, getting more private by the day. Only Zora stays at the table, head in her plump little hands, guarding the tea tray.

We sip and talk over the details of the grand plan that makes adults of Arend and me. I suppose he was one already. But I feel I have graduated today.

'I'm toying with plans to make a fish smoker,' says my brother. 'When I have a good catch I could smoke some and sell some. Just a theory at the moment, to keep on the backburner.'

Dad seems a bit exhausted now that it's all been discussed. 'Time will tell what the main stay of this farm will be. For the moment it's still wheat and sheep and all the rest is gravy. But that could change. It has to change.'

'And if we want to make good use of the fruit trees we already have,' I suggest, 'we should practise drying apricots, peaches and apples this summer. You can dry them on sheets of corrugated iron under a piece of thin cloth and store them in jars. Or in sealed pastic bags to sell.'

'In that case, Arend and I must look into hammering together some stormproof racks to hold the iron sheets,' says Dad. 'Anchor them down on the long side of the shed. I suppose we'll need a tarpaulin on hand in case of sudden downpours. Anything we learn this summer will come in handy later. Let's give that one a go.' He's keen as mustard now to start re-inventing the farm.

'Okay. And where's that little pair of scales that used to sit on the kitchen bench?' I ask. 'I'll need it to weigh seeds in packets of ten grams or whatever. I have an idea for making the packets myself. It won't cost more than a pot of glue.'

'Those scales are in the bottom cupboard,' says Mum. 'They're all yours, I never use them.'

'I think it's really efficient to build two houses and a shop in one go,' says Arend. 'Once we get into our stride it will become daily routine. Not that I'm setting time limits, neither is Bianka. We'll do what we can when we can.'

'Fair dinkum,' Dad sighs, 'but we'll be going full bore in the next twelve months. No sleeping in when the rain pours down, there'll be a multitude of things to do in the shed like never before! And when the mercury hits forty we may be up to our necks in fruit, so we'd better put the old fridge back into service in the shed. We ought to have monthly meetings like this one and can somebody make a list of all the things to do, please?'

'I will tonight,' says Arend. 'After I've taken Whoopsy for a gallop to the new building site. I want to make a sketch to take to the draughtsman. We'll have to submit a proper plan to council. Wonder what that'll cost.'

'Don't worry,' growls Auntie Branka. Is she rich? Or is she using up her last savings to be a full partner? What would we do without her?

'I'm going to jot a few business ideas down on paper,' I tell the family and leave them to the dregs of Zora's teapot.

15: Roll Out the Future

In the bottom of my wardrobe sits a cardboard box with scrap drawing paper from a Queenscape printer who offloaded it at school. We were allowed to take as much as we wanted and I must have been a greedy guts, for I never used even a tenth of it. Now I take a closer look. It's strong quality paper in large sheets. The printing is on one side, all mixed up. Proofs for something that went wrong. No white. There's bright blue, lemon and green. Excellent. I take a sheet and draw the outline of a seed packet on the blank side. With a fine felt pen I draw fancy lettering in an arch across the top:

BIANKA'S SEEDS
Native Seeds from
PLATYPUS ISLAND
10 grams of
. . . .
RSD via
Queenscape P.I.

Cutting out the packet with a back, top and side flaps, I fold it and presto! A lick of glue and I'm in business, making sure those corners don't leak seed. I wonder how much the printer will charge to print four packets to a sheet. I'll put my own money into this if necessary. And I will handwrite the species names on each packet, artistically of course. Or, I could write every packet by hand until I make profits. Why not? Three coloured pens and a few evenings work. I'll start production tomorrow!

I wonder whether collecting wattle seed at twenty dollars a kilo might be slave labour. It's used as bush tucker. But it is also the preferred food of galahs, corellas and other birds I don't want to deprive, wasteful eaters though they are. I suppose I could just harvest a tree or two for our own use.

On another sheet I design my hut. How large shall I make my room? What shape the seed room? A seed room needs to be dry and cool, so it could face east with an overhanging verandah. Might as well run that around the whole house. A thin room across the width of the hut would be handy, with wooden shelves divided into compartments for at least a hundred varieties of seed. There are lots of planks in the shed and I can paint them different colours for trees, shrubs and groundcovers. Hey! Green, blue and yellow to match the packets!

A long workbench for sorting and packing and a card system in a shoebox to keep track of what I collect. An accounts book and a customers book. How to get customers? Advertise? Ask the council? Look in magazines in the library? That's the scary part. What if I collect all this seed and can't sell it? I think of Jason and our pact. I must work for it, find out how to organise sales. Other people learn those things and so can I. The whole world is trading and so can I.

Last of all I sketch my dream room, door and window facing the sea and my imaginary island where so many of my dreams have ended up. My bed with the log-cabin quilt against the dividing wall. Table at the window with plant books, sketch book, pencils, pens. Me sitting there looking out to sea, thinking about life, my business and Jason. Having breakfast there. At night I'll sit on the verandah watching the sea go dark as the sun sets into the restless water. Sometimes the moon bathes everything in a silver glow. And when Jason comes back we'll watch the sun and moon together.

Could I build an open fireplace with a chimney for cold evenings? Do I need other bricks for that? Check out. What about the floor? Hardpacked dirt is cheapest. I'm not fussed. I could buy two comfy secondhand chairs at the dealers for ten bucks, ask Mum to run me up some cushions and stuff them with fleece. One wall-to-wall rod in a corner will hang my clothes.

What about cooking or do I keep eating with the family? I'll want to be independent when I feel like it. A table with primus against the north wall. A cutting-board, pots and pans, mugs and plates. Start with the minimum, don't clutter the place. There are enough spare utensils and furniture in our home to outfit my hut. Need a bin with a lid to keep bread and things that mice will eat.

I love it! I colour three lines on the plan where the

seed shelves are, then draw red squares for furniture. My own hut. My hermit's hut. Bianka's Seed business in Anka's hut. My hermit name is Anka.

∽

Arend and I just hung up the day's washing and he's off to peg out the site of his house. I wake up with such excitement these days – about Jason, our pact, my hut and my status as partner in the farm. The phone rings and it is an enquiry for a booking. Pretty early in the day – must be a working person.

'We have direct acces to the beach,' I tell the lady. 'Two beautiful rooms with an enclosed verandah to sit in. Breakfast and dinner and optional packed lunches. Most of the food is grown on the farm – we make our own honey and sheep cheese.' I rave on a bit about swimming, fishing, exploring and the seals. She asks about rates for two adults and two kids for two weeks in December and says she'll ring back. Sometimes they do and sometimes they don't. It's like that. I am beginning to feel like a real business woman. Using my own initiative. After all, I'm one of the partners.

Arend comes back with mail at ten, plonks it in the middle of the table and says: 'Letter for you, sis,' giving me a look.

Flustered, I move to the table. Can it be? Whoever writes to me? Arend pushes a long white envelope across. I pick it up. 'Miss Bianka Woodsman'. I turn it over. My heart leaps as I read: 'Jason Jacobs, c/o

School of Martial Arts'. The letter feels as solid as Jason's arm. Not like Flora. He really exists. He wasn't something I dreamed up.

'See you later, alligator,' I say to Arend. He smirks. I'm off to my room where I carefully slit the envelope and take out a typed sheet of paper.

Dear Bianka,

How are you? I'm back in the fray, but good memories from the holiday keep me sane. As promised, I spoke to my sister and brother-in-law about your wish to learn self-defence in a jiffy. We talked it through from all angles and the three of us have come up with a plan. It goes like this:

There are two evening classes a week teaching self-defence for women, which you should definitely take. The other nights there are mixed classes of martial arts which you should watch, until you can try some of it in the junior section. During the day, assuming you're coming over to learn self-defence intensively, you can assist my sister Rebecca with several mothers and children's classes and after-school sessions run by Beckie and Damien together.

You'll learn a great deal this way, assisting and participating. You only pay for the women's self-defence classes, see enclosed price list. The rest you sort of work for, as Beckie could really do with an assistant for a spell.

About accommodation. Maybe you'll want to find your own, but my sister and brother-in-law make you this offer: there are several small store rooms on the second floor, hardly used. You can have one of them with a camp bed if you bring a sleeping-bag. It'll be like camping, but dry! We all live in the building, so it won't be too lonely. You eat with the family in return for chipping in with the cooking. I told Beckie what a great cook you are and she flipped. She can't wait for you to get here, because she's been having a hard time of it since the teaching started expanding – and with two schoolgoing kids.

One more thing. They both say you cannot hope to learn enough in five days, as you planned. You have to come for at least three weeks. That will give you a good basis for your purposes and then, if you practise at home, you can come back periodically for a week's extension course. How does that sound?

Write when you want to come. Doesn't matter when. If you come before Christmas, I will still be here. Could you come early December? Or even November? Pack your bags almost straight away?

Bianka, please discuss this letter with your parents and let me know if they want Beckie to give them a ring, to assure them we will all look after you like one of the family. To save time, ring me as soon as you can. Mostly home evenings after six. Exams just starting, so I'm swotting.

Speak to you soon.

Jason.

After 'Speak to you soon' he has drawn a little folded flower with round petals, a quince flower. I turn hot and cold as I read the letter again. There's a lot between the lines that he could not write, because I have to discuss the letter with Mum and Dad. He wants me to come. He wants to have me around for three whole weeks even though he's swotting! Be a part of his family. I am going. I am going in November, before that new booking happens, if it does. I have the Sea Horse ticket, enough savings for the women's self-defence course, and I can earn my keep. Wow! What an opportunity!

But for my pact partner Jason, my wish to learn martial arts would still be a wish. How can I return this favour? Ah, I can always offer him a holiday on Platypus, since I'm a partner in Woodsman's Homestead Guesthouse!

I escape the house to work in the vegetable garden, find space to calm my excited heart. Chugging a hoe through rows of young cabbages and cauliflowers, I move mentally between kids doing martial arts movements. I'll do it intensive all right. The only other thing I will do in the city is check out plant books in bookshops. Then I can mail order titles as I earn money from selling seeds. Bliss. I let my mind go blank, up and down with the hoe, bending and stretching to pick up clods of weeds. Where do city people go to think or stop thinking? You'd have to have a garden if you lived there, or go mad.

The plots are buzzing with bees collecting nectar from flowering winter vegetables about to set seed: broccoli, bok choy, rocket and swedes. If I spread compost around the new stakes Arend put in after the storm, I can plant beans today. Radishes too. The pumpkin mounds sport little vines reaching out in all directions. Put more in if we are going to have so many guests. Not too late. The whole food garden has to become more intensive to cope with those invasions. Stand-by vegies. Silverbeet for spinach pies. Cabbages for coleslaw. More caulies, everyone loves cauliflower bake with sheep cheese. Get seedlings for cucumbers, capsicums and tomatoes this week. The weather is warming up.

Who will water my garden when I'm away? But don't I have six partners in this business, not counting Auntie Branka? They can take turns to do it! We need a roster board in the kitchen. I hope no one objects to me going. There were no murmurs when I won the Sea Horse ticket. But what will they think of me moving in with Jason's family?

Before I return to the house I hook the old basket off its pole to pull carrots and a resprouted onion, pick a stalk of rocket, a bunch of silverbeet and a handful of coriander. I'll make a carrot and coriander salad in orange juice. And a big spinach quiche, with pasta in sautéed onion, rocket on top. A few meatballs and dinner is done!

Must collect the eggs and give the flock this bucket

of succulent weeds. The geese have started their second round of spring eggs, still hoping for goslings, poor things. Maybe I should get fertilised eggs so they can do the natural thing and go broody? We have the space. Or should I go for more ducks with a longer laying season? Poor birds, all we humans think of is how to exploit them. They never intended to lay all those eggs for people.

'Here Dora Duck, Daisy Duck, Della Duck! Mother Goose, Gilly Goose, Gail Goose! Romeo! All you chookies! Here's your grub.' They never fight over weeds, grass or vegetable scraps, only over apple peel. Bread or grain turn them wildly competitive. Dora chases Della who finds a slug in the weeds and runs with it. What a way to go. Nature is not kind.

For a few minutes I watch their little rituals. The geese carry tufts of grass to the water trough to carefully wash out any dirt before eating. The ducks drill their beaks into the soft ground by the tap as if digging up weeds themselves. And Romeo does his usual soft shuffle invitation to dinner before he scratches the ground with his mighty claws as his flock gathers around. Only then does he take a peck himself. Just like Dad, who never starts eating until we are all at the table, no matter how hungry and worn-out he may be.

The food garden sits on a slight rise, so I can see a good part of the farm from here. How beautiful it is, my home island. The trees, green fields and busy birds, the woolly dots in the far paddock where our sheep are grazing this week. Even the buildings, simple as they are, have old-world charm, as the visitors say when they photograph them. The big iron shed still has dew running down one side. The hay shed, machine shed and little silo each have a character all their own. And our sprawling homestead with its wrap-around verandah nestles in a ring of wattle and scrub with just a few patches of flowers maintained by Mum. Her daisies, carnations and rose bushes sit in wide borders of soft grey lambs' ear and wormwood.

To the south the land rises slowly and you cannot see the new strip from here. That's what is so good about it. My hut will be hidden from view, yet close to all this. I walk back to the house, at peace.

∽

My birthday fell on Thursday and we baked as usual, including my choice of cheese cake. The celebration took place after dinner. I felt silly blowing out eighteen candles, but terribly good about being eighteen just the same.

With a lot of chuckles Mum and Dad gave me a small suitcase and matching overnight bag. 'This is no hint, daughter!' grinned Dad, 'we just want you to know that we trust you will travel. You may even have to travel for your business in years to come.' So sweet!

Auntie Branka gave me an envelope with more than a card in it. Spending money! She really knows my needs. And Arend and the littlies bunched together with a gorgeous kimono and nightie in lemon and peach. I bet Coral did the choosing for she'd love it herself. The family did real fast work after I told them I'd be going to the School of Martial Arts in November. They must have hit the phone and the agents, but everything arrived in time. I'm all set to go.

I didn't have a girls' party this year and Sylvie forgot because of exams, so that's fine. I'm too busy myself. Jason sent a funny birthday card. We spoke on the phone after his letter. I was nervous as a rabbit, thinking it was never going to be like cave days again. But as soon as I heard his voice shouting: 'Hey Quince Flower! When are you coming?' I knew everything was right as rain.

It has all been arranged. The days are still routine, but I have driving lessons with Arend every day to get that under my belt before I turn my attention to martial arts. Every spare moment I'm making seed packets – they're looking real artistic. Or I'm ringing the library or walking the scrub, book in hand to identify species. My hut plan is stuck on my door so I can pencil in changes before laying out the ground plan around Christmas. The December booking came through and Mum was so pleased for the money, but after they're gone I will lay the first stone!

Woodsman's Homestead will feature in the new edition of *Secrets of Platypus Island*. Auntie growled:

'What secrets? They're telling all!' But I know there are secrets on Platypus no visitor is likely to stumble on. Mum and Dad speculate on having visitors all summer, with luck.

Arend is already clearing the site for his house and shop. You can find him and Dad drawing mud maps almost daily, discussing a door here and a downpipe there.

Auntie is spinning and knitting like fury – she's packed the first pairs of finished socks in cellophane bags. If she's not in the cheese room, Mum sits at the sewing machine enjoying herself with her latest quilt. Coral was reading cookbooks instead of doing homework until I warned her to make sure she passes to Year Eleven or she'll be at school another year!

Yvan pesters Arend every day for driving lessons. And gorgeous Zora solemnly makes tea after school, swinging an old cowbell at the back door to ring in the troops. Poor old Dad seems to be running the farm almost single-handed again. On top of it all he works on new things like the lean-to for my temporary seed storage, the first fruit-drying rack and the mud bricks production line. But they are one-off jobs and we all seem to have more energy.

There is a new spirit about the house. I am almost sorry to leave. But it's only for three weeks and I will be with Jason.

16: Sweet Independence

It seems as if I've been away three months instead of three weeks. Life at the School of Martial Arts was so different that it blew my mind – the pace was exhilarating. Yet, family life was much the same. The kids, Tony and Mandy, squabbling before school and after. Washing day, shopping day, all that. From late morning till bedtime, except for the breaks, I was in the big gym working on my mat or helping out with classes.

At first my muscles protested, but Beckie gave me massage until I got used to such intense physical activity. It was fun helping juniors and I almost wished for a career with small children. But the thought of my hut and the sea and the family partnership won out. I've enjoyed kids unlimited for a few weeks, but always?

Jason was swotting endlessly. If he wasn't doing exams he sat in his room buried in books. He used to do martial arts a lot, but had to neglect it for studies. He will take it up again in Canberra to keep up with me! When he came out of his room for coffee or a quick lunch, he'd often sit with his arm around my shoulders as if we were in the cave.

I joined him in eating vegetarian style and I'm going to try to keep off meat at home, because I really feel for the animals being slaughtered. Jason says the world population could be fed better if we ate the crops instead of feeding them to cattle or letting them graze the earth bare. But fish, often on the table at home, is the most natural of foods for islanders. So I may become a hypocrite. Our fish have had a free life before they're landed. Then again, I love vegetables. I must sort this out before I turn twenty-one. Decisions …

One day Jason said to Beckie: 'This island flower saved my sanity, Beck. When I went on holiday I was still pretty confused and scatterbrained. Then I watched her going about her work day in, day out and something clicked in my stupid head. She is an amazing person who knows exactly what she wants and goes after it. Like doing martial arts in a hurry. So I made a pact with her, to save myself.'

He laughed and squeezed my shoulder and Beckie smiled, taking it all with a grain of salt. But one day she said to me: 'Bianka, I don't know what your secret is, but my brother seems so mature lately, even wise. Keep doing what you're doing.'

All this is a mystery to me. I didn't know myself what I wanted to do when Jason came to Platypus. I have no secret powers over him. I thought he was awfully mature when I first met him. Alone with him one afternoon I mentioned these things. He gave me a long look before saying: 'Quince Flower, what all this means is that you and I are good for each other. Together we are more than the sum total of each of

174

us apart. Please keep the pact. I need it. You need it. And I need you, my island girl.'

He gave me a featherlight kiss on the mouth. He looked so tired then, his eyes red. He sat his last exam the day before I was leaving and that evening we all went to a Japanese restaurant to celebrate. Jason was almost too tired to eat, but so happy. 'It's gone better than any other year,' he said, 'thanks to Bianka being here to inspire me.'

I'm not even embarrassed any more when he says these things, because I know he means them. It is true, we are good for each other. When I just think of Jason, I feel I can do anything. He was so proud of my achievements in the school when Damien told him I was a natural with martial arts.

We managed to snatch bits of time to talk. I told him of Flora's other ribbon and how the three ribbons connect us and the cave. He listened so quietly to the story of Flora's life, then said it accounted for a sort of shadow he always imagined seeing behind me. He'd been worried about that impression, thinking it was that Byderdike rat stalking me. But now he was sure it was Flora's 'substance' as my ancestor and the fact I carried her in the forefront of my mind. With Jason you can talk about mysteries!

I said I'd like to search for Great-uncle Frederik one day and Jason immediately looked up Queensland phonebooks on the internet and there it was: F. Hammermeyer and his address! It gave me cold shivers! I decided to send him a Christmas card explaining who I am. He may not want to know our family any more and I would respect that. But he may want to read his mother's diary.

Jason talked again about me going to university. I'm scared, I guess, but he reckons I would love the university library and studying really interesting subjects of my own choosing. I asked him whether he was thinking of Adelaide, and he was. 'But,' he said, 'if you decided to come to Canberra I would be over the moon.'

I was terribly torn and Jason saw it. 'I'd love to just study botany and another language,' I said. 'And I wonder whether the university library has Flora's books.'

'I'll check for Flora's books,' Jason said, hugging me. 'And for the rest, let's go with the flow this coming year. So much is happening for you and me and us. This time next year we'll have a conference about the future, in the cave.' We kissed on that, to seal the pact again.

This week he's off to Canberra to find a flat for Stephen and himself. Back for Christmas with his family, then Canberra, for two or three years. But he'll come to Platypus during first semester holidays, traveling on a student bus ticket from Canberra. I feel proud he's taking the ferry just to see me. I promised to feed him the best of the leftovers. Jason won't be a paying guest any more! From now on he's my guest.

'I can't live a whole year on letters,' he moaned. 'I was stupid to make a pact that says we can only write when we're in trouble.'

'We can change the rules,' I said. 'We are in charge of the pact.'

So we pledged to write whenever we feel like it. Pledged again with ceremony on a smooth pebble that sat on Beckie's windowsill between the potplants.

'And something else,' he said. 'When I figure out what times of day I am free to think of you, I'll write and let you know. If you can think of me at the same times, we will be in touch every day. Let's see what happens then!'

'What's the time difference between Canberra and here?' I asked.

'That depends – winter or summer. I'll ring you from there when to start. It probably has to be early morning.'

'And for weekends we can set a time when I go to the cave and you'll know I'll be there.'

'Only when the sea isn't rough. Don't you go clambering rocks in a storm to keep a date with Jason's ghost!'

All this we decided as Jason drove me in the dark before dawn to the Sea Horse bus that connects with the ferry. He waited till the bus left and I waved until it turned a corner. Then I experienced a dreadfully empty feeling for what seemed ages – the bottom fell out of my life. But I knew he might feel the same and we shouldn't. So I went over the whole conversation again, word for word, again and again, until I knew it off by heart. Then I memorised other conversations we had in Beckie's kitchen, even back on Platypus. I did this all the way to the Cape where the boat lay in the morning light, and across the strait until the Sea Horse bumped to a stop against the quay at Queenscape, where Dad and Arend waited for me.

I was so thrilled to see them that I told them all I'd learned there and then. And then a most amazing thing happened. Dad and Arend went into the hardware store to buy grommets for the fruit-rack tarp. I got out of the truck to walk fifty metres to the shore, just enjoying the sight of big water and the smell of salt after those city fumes.

As I stood there with my hands in my pockets, the hairs on my neck suddenly prickled and I got that ominous cold feeling down the length of my spine. I swung around quick as lightning, hands out of my pockets and stretched, like I'd just learned in martial arts and it was second nature now. And who stood there leering at me from the opposite pavement? That rat Patrick Byderdike!

I don't know what got into me, but I started crossing the road and made for him. But before I was halfway, he turned and walked away quicker than I've ever seen the slink move on. He disappeared around the corner without looking back even once. When I reached the spot where he'd been leering, I picked up a sudden fear. I knew that wasn't mine. There was no fear in me whatsoever. It was his. Blow me down! I scared that slimy pervert into taking to his heels!

When Dad and Arend came back we went for coffee on the deck of Jetty's Café and I sort of told them what just happened. I didn't brag and I didn't tell them of smelling that fear hanging above the pavement. Just told them what I did. Actually, I'd done nothing – just moved to hunt the slink.

Arend said: 'Good on you, sis. You keep that up.' But Dad looked at me in amazement before finally asking: 'How dangerous have you become, I wonder, daughter of mine?'

Arend and I kidded him. We teased him that I could swing him onto the truck like Bruce Lee does, before I assured him: 'Dad, it's only dangerous to someone who wants to harm me. I've learned to defend myself against attackers, but I may never need to use it at all!'

'Not if you can scare a man off the streets just by giving him a look and swinging your arms from that sort of distance!' Dad said. He was clearly impressed and it made me feel amazingly good.

We checked at the council when the building licences would be approved. Soon, the clerk told us. He didn't think there would be any problems for them going through. I hadn't seen the drawing the draughtsman had made from my sketch, but Arend said he'd just made the hut wider and adjusted the pitch of the roof to withstand southern storms.

While we were there, Dad heard that the resort development wasn't going through after all. The consortium couldn't raise the money and the land is up for sale again. We were smugly pleased. Locals are still talking about buying it together and setting up a model farm for agriculture students and mainland school camps. A great idea.

Coming home was more wonderful than I could have imagined. It was late afternoon by the time we pulled in, loaded with building materials, bags of fertiliser and the supplies. Mum had baked a chocolate cake for my homecoming and Zora brewed the tea. Auntie Branka sat at her wheel, spinning like fury. Everyone asked questions as I told about my other life, showing them a defending pose and taking Yvan in a hold he couldn't worm out of. Boy, did he hate that! I can see him take up the art just to save face.

I got a lump in my throat when Zora and Yvan clung to me shouting: 'What did you bring us, Bianka?' Sometimes it's nice to be elder sister. I'd bought books for everyone at a shop Jason knew, where they are half price. Used all the money Auntie Branka gave me and bought some terrific plant books as well.

At mealtime I told them about wanting to skip meat from now on and Dad said: 'We'll respect that, won't we Tinka?' Mum nodded and I will never know what she thought of it. No one else made any remarks at all. It's nice to be treated as an adult.

I had a wonderful sleep in my own bed after listening to the wind, waking up this morning to the creaking of the verandah, still dreaming of Jason. When daylight came and breakfast was done, I was given a quick tour of the farm by Dad and Arend.

The progress has been incredible. Both building sites have been smoothed flat by one of Dad's bulldozer friends. Two rows of strong young apricot trees stand in nicely dug earth with mulch, not far from the sheds and protected from wind by the scrub. Dad explained how Arend came up with a solution for the bird problem. In the second year, when we expect fruit, he and Dad will built a netting cage around the trees, with a removable flap on one side. On that side they can extend the plantings next autumn with twenty olive trees and twenty almond trees. The cage gets extended year by year as the trees come into fruit.

'So we can pickle olives galore for the visitors and ourselves?' I ask.

'And press virgin olive oil,' says Arend. 'And maybe almond oil. I'm negotiating with the museum for two old millstones, small ones. They have at least a dozen there. I'm trying to convince the board that they should be brought back in production to help make farms more viable.'

'Coral will be able to do some authentic Mediterranean cooking.'

'Yeh,' says Dad, 'and them oils are good for your

heart, I hear. Better than bacon and butter. So we'll press for family provisions first, that's our new principle. If we work harder we must also be in the peak of health.'

Dear Dad has changed. He's talking like a young man with ideals. That he has been working flat out is visible everywhere. Two drying racks stand bolted to the shed, each capable of holding eight corrugated iron sheets, enough for a tonne of fruit! Dad never does things by halves. He has also ploughed up experimental legume plots. The cheese room has a tiny new cultivation tank 'for Mum to try her hand at yoghurt just for us', he says.

Somewhere Arend found an old telephone booth for nothing if he would haul it away. It stands bold and red in a cleared spot and will become his fish smoker. Selfsufficiency has just about arrived!

Dad somehow found space in the laundry to hammer together another large cupboard. He and Arend raided every op shop on the island for preserving jars and stored them on the new shelves, ready for chutneys and pickles. Next week the four guests arrive and we shift around, but I won't have to do any of it. And we have two bookings already for high summer, one week each.

Auntie Branka and Mum seem like women possessed. They sit together in the livingroom, cutting, sewing, spinning, knitting and listening to talkback radio and criticising most of it, while the birds chirrup through the open windows. Coral has apparently made her revolting apricot chutney recipe with dried apricots and convinced the family she knows what she's doing.

Everybody is frantically creating something, except Yvan whose time hasn't yet come. As usual, he tries to escape anything that smells faintly like work. But the partnership is obviously working. The mood is great, we talk endlessly at mealtimes, and nobody says 'no' if you ask for something involving the new plans.

One evening Dad discusses with us that all the new things we are doing may not work out one hundred per cent. Therefore we must keep our eyes and ears open for other projects the farm could support. That's exciting, like a business constantly moving into new ventures, shedding redundant projects, taking on new challenges. But everything is limited by how hard we work, running so many projects simultaneously. And by how much capital Auntie Branka can invest.

I rang Sylvie. Told her I'd been learning martial arts at a friend's place. She was depressed about her matric exams. 'But even if I fail I'll still go to the mainland,' she said. 'I'll take any old job and do courses at TAFE and live with my auntie until I'm financial and then I'll get my own flat. I'm not going to be a sitting duck here on the island for hordes of blokes who can't find girlfriends!'

She's right. There have been reports in the *Platypus Argus* about girls becoming so scarce on the island that guys are going across to find wives! All because of the crisis in farming, not helped by frequent droughts. Eldest sons stay on, trying to keep farms going. But more than half the girls leave because there are no jobs for them. A few come back as nurses and teachers, but the rest marry on the mainland and only come home for Christmas.

I told Sylvie about the family partnership and getting my own business, small as it is. 'Gosh!' she sighed and fell a bit silent. I realise it could never happen in her family.

'But how can you ever make enough money from all these little products?' she finally asked. 'Like how are you ever going to have a car of your own? Or nice clothes? Or money for travel? I couldn't live on a shoestring forever, I'm sick of it now!'

I admitted we didn't expect to be rolling in money. 'But we've made a decision as a family that we're not after money, but after a good life,' I tried to tell her. 'And I can perhaps earn enough to travel to the mainland for business sometimes. I know that's no great shakes, but living away can be lonely and expensive too. I realised that when I was in the city those three weeks. If I hadn't had my friend's family, I would have been miserable.'

But Sylvie was not impressed. She's hell-bent on leaving and that may be the end of our close friendship. I'll really be Anka the Hermit. But I have Jason and he's enough. Poor Arend, another girl leaving

Platypus. Sylvie is hardly the type to keep shop at our gateway!

♋

I'm sitting in the cave in my adventure suit because it's Saturday. The waves are calm, the tide out and I'm thinking of Jason. Soon we will set times to contact each other here. I crawl to the back of the cave. Flora's ribbon still lies where Jason left it. Well, it's been here half a century. But it amazes me that just touching it creates such a link with the past that I feel anchored and secure. I know she would approve of my learning martial arts. And she would have loved seeing me chase Patrick Byderdike off the pavement, tail between his legs.

Wouldn't Flora just adore Jason. He'd be the sort of man she ought to have lived with – original, humorous, romantic, loyal, supportive and bursting with ideas. I think she'd be pleased if she could see me here, in the cave where she took her leave of Platypus Island and her dream island out there in the ocean. Again I wonder why she left her hat. Was she caught out by the tide and forgot it as she hurried back? Or did she drop it on purpose, leaving something of herself in a place she loved, or where Tom might one day find it? Poor Flora, romance withered on the vine of her life. But it has returned to mine.

As I climb back across the boulders the sun catches the sheen on the wing of a small plane flying over. The beam is reflected by something far out at sea, bouncing back like a signal, straight into my eyes. Yet, there's nothing to be seen there – not a sail, nor the short dark line of a ship on the horizon. Sometime Island is but a dream. It has been my refuge for a very long time, but lately it has receded and today I cannot visualise it vividly at all. Three months ago my life was at a complete standstill, but now, standing in the same place as then, all my dreams are coming together here on Platypus Island.

Slowly I walk to the site of Anka's Hut, carrying a big, beautiful pebble that stared me in the eye from between the rocks. White and maroon veins are embedded in the grey stone, worn smooth by the waves of the Great Southern Ocean. I place the stone where the corner of Anka's Hut will be. Walking towards the homestead, I turn to look back at that corner stone. It sits there solitary, solo and at home.